ROADSIDE ATTRACTION

M.G. Higgins

SADDLEBACK
EDUCATIONAL PUBLISHING

Gravel Road

Bi-Normal
Edge of Ready
Expecting *(rural)*
Falling Out of Place
FatherSonFather
Finding Apeman *(rural)*
A Heart Like Ringo
  Starr *(verse)*
I'm Just Me
Otherwise *(verse)*
Roadside Attraction *(rural)*

Rodeo Princess *(rural)*
Screaming Quietly
Self. Destructed.
Skinhead Birdy
Sticks and Stones *(rural)*
Teeny Little Grief
  Machines *(verse)*
That Selfie Girl *(verse)*
2 Days
Unchained
Varsity 170

SADDLEBACK
EDUCATIONAL PUBLISHING
www.sdlback.com

ISBN-13: 978-1-68021-102-3
ISBN-10: 1-68021-102-1
eBook: 978-1-63078-399-0

Printed in China
NOR/0316/CA21600430

20 19 18 17 16   1 2 3 4 5

Chapter 1

My dad always says, "You've seen one cactus. You've seen them all."

I get his point. But at least the cactus are interesting. More interesting than the plants where we live. Knee-high brush that's kindling by August.

Tumbling tumbleweeds.

Those are words from an old song. The kind of music my grandparents play at their store. Like there's something romantic about tumbleweeds. Stuck in cattle fences, jammed under junk cars.

I don't like disagreeing with my dad. But I like cactus. Especially saguaros, the tall green ones I'm driving by right now. They look like giant cactus people. Arms out. Palms up. Like they're being arrested. "Stick 'em up, cactus *hombre*." Mom took me to a park around here when I was ten. There were a zillion of them. A cactus convention.

The highway curves and the cactus people disappear.

Tucson recedes in my rearview mirror. Traffic thins out. Now it's just me. Semis. RVs. Cars loaded with tents and suitcases. Kids in the backseat, whining, "Are we there yet?"

All those travelers equal money in my grandparents' pockets. Which equals money in my pockets. So I don't complain. I like the money I make. Can't wait to spend it on something now that I've graduated.

The landscape turns flat and barren. Distant mountains. Tumbleweeds not tumbling in the hot still air.

An hour later things get rockier. The signs start showing up. *Geronimo's Last Stand! Ten Miles Ahead!*

Two miles later: *Geronimo's Last Stand! See History! Gas! Sodas! Snacks! Souvenirs!*

I've just passed *Authentic Mexican Pottery! Geronimo's Last Stand! 2 Miles!* when I see a hitchhiker. Short cut-off jeans. Backpack. Thumb out.

Our eyes meet as I drive by. She's young, maybe fourteen or fifteen. Frowning. Short black hair with blue streaks. Flip-flops. No hat. It's over a hundred degrees. What is she thinking?

There's no way I'm picking her up. Never picked up a hitchhiker. Never will. I've heard too many horror stories. Seen too many freaky movies.

I turn up the radio. Flex my fingers around the steering wheel. Reach the final billboard two miles later. *Geronimo's Last Stand. THIS EXIT!!!! TURN NOW!!!!*

I turn and take the exit. But not because the sign tells me to.

I belong here.

The parking lot is full. Gas pumps busy. The facade of the convenience store looks like a town from the Old West. It's just a front. Fake. Supposed to add to the old-timey atmosphere.

I drive to the rear. Park next to the loading door. Grab two cardboard boxes from the back of the pickup and carry them to the storeroom.

Grandpa meets me there. "Hey, Logan. Did they hassle you about the return?"

"No, they were cool."

He grabs the box cutter from the workbench. Cuts through the packing tape and pulls out a T-shirt. It's bright blue. Outline of Geronimo's face in dark green. Green lettering underneath. *Geronimo's Last Stand. Ferris, Arizona.*

He studies it and nods. "Better than the last batch." He opens the other box. "Did you go see your mom?"

"No."

"But you said—"

"I never said anything. You assumed, like always."

He sighs and shakes his head. Pulls out a baseball cap. Same blue as the shirts. Same lettering and image. "Stock a few shirts in the store, will you? Especially extra large. We sold the last one this morning. Then we can use your help at the registers. I need to watch for a delivery."

I carry a bunch of T-shirts into the store. Stack them on the shelves. The clothing aisle is near the restrooms. A string of women line up outside the ladies room. That's why most people stop here—to pee. But almost no one leaves without buying something, even if it's just a soda. Bag of chips. And they want to see Geronimo's Last Stand, of course. All those billboards stoke their curiosity.

"Logan!" Grandma waves me over to the counter. Customers wait six deep behind her register.

I go over and help her. "Where's Dad?"

"Taking a break."

Dad needs a lot of breaks. He's not really suited for this kind of work. But there's not a lot else he can do. "Is he okay?" I ask.

"Just a bad day."

I shouldn't have gone to Tucson. It upset his routine.

I notice Melody get in my line. She's holding Hannah, her baby daughter.

"I can help you over here, sweetie," Grandma says to her. My line's moving slower.

"That's okay, Mrs. Monroe." Melody flashes her sweet smile that makes my insides melt. Her light brown hair is pulled back in her summer ponytail.

I finish with my customer. Melody sets a Diet Coke

on the counter. Bag of pretzels. She shifts Hannah on her hip.

"No Snickers today?" I ask.

"I'm on a diet."

"You're kidding."

"I've turned pudgy since Hannah, as if you haven't noticed. Hey, have you heard from Seth?"

I shake my head.

"Neither have we. Thought he might have texted you."

"He just left Sunday. I'm giving him a chance to settle in," I say.

"That's what I told Mom and Dad. But …" she shrugs. "They worry."

I give Melody her change.

"You working here all summer?" she asks.

"Nothing else to do. Not with Seth at baseball camp." I bag her stuff. Hand it to her.

"Well, see you around," she says.

"Right. See you later."

My eyes linger on her as she leaves with Hannah. She's not fat. She's perfect. A girl passes them coming into the store. Black hair with blue streaks. Cut-off blue jeans. Flip-flops.

The hitchhiker.

She scans us. I don't think she recognizes me. Not that she would. I drove by at eighty miles an hour. She's carrying that big backpack. Perfect for shoplifting.

The registers have slowed. "Think I'll follow that one," I whisper to Grandma.

She studies the girl, same as I did. "Might want to get your dad up here first."

I head to the staff room. It's just a small space with a couch and card table. Coffee maker and small refrigerator. Broken souvenirs, or ones that never sold—fake kachina dolls, fake Indian blankets. A desert wildflower poster. Dad's sitting at the table, hands folded in front of him. He jerks his head up when I walk in. Gives me a relieved smile. "You're back."

"Of course I'm back. Feel good enough to go up front?"

"Sure. Is it busy?"

"Not bad. Possible shoplifter I need to watch."

"Then go ahead." His knees shake as he gets to his feet.

"Are you sure? I can drive you home."

"I'm fine!"

I give him a final glance before I go to the storeroom. Grab a handful of baseball caps. They'll give me a reason to walk the aisles.

I look up at the fish-eye mirror near the ceiling. Don't see the girl. Maybe she's in the restroom. I stock the caps on the shelf, next to the snow globes and collector spoons. She leaves the restroom just as I finish. I wander slowly behind her.

A car backfires outside.

Someone screams.

It's Dad.

Chapter 2

I rush to the counter. Dad's crouched on the floor, trembling so hard I think he might fly apart.

Grandpa's down there with him, his hand on Dad's back. "It's all right, Jimmy. It's all right." Grandpa coos like he's talking to an infant.

I'd ask what happened, but I know. Dad was having a bad day. Already stressed. The backfire sent him over the edge.

I move to go help them, but Grandma grabs my arm. "He's okay," she whispers. "Best not pay him too much attention."

She's right. It will just embarrass him more. I take a deep breath. Try to calm my pounding heart. Get behind a register. Wait on the next customer while still keeping an eye on Dad. Grandpa helps him up. Leads him back to the staff room. Customers stare and murmur to each other.

Then I remember. Hitchhiker. I glance in the mirror. She's at the cooler, slipping a bottle into her backpack.

Damn it.

I quickly finish with my customer. "I'll be right back," I tell Grandma.

"Can you wait until Grandpa gets here?"

"No."

The girl is out the door already. Walking fast. I trot after her. "Hey."

She turns and eyes me. Keeps walking. She's past the gas pumps now, at the dirt strip near the access road.

"Hey!" I shout. "Stop!"

She stops but doesn't turn. I step in front of her. Her nose, cheeks, and forehead glow red with sunburn. Her brown eyes shoot sparks at me. "What?" she spits out.

"I saw you slip a bottle into your backpack. You didn't to pay for it."

"Are you a cop?"

"No. It's my store."

She looks me up and down. "*Your* store?"

"Close enough. Give me what you took and I won't call the sheriff."

She rolls her eyes. Stands there a second, deciding what to do. Finally she sets down her pack. Leans over and unzips it. Takes out a water bottle. Candy bar. Tuna sandwich. Bag of nuts. Sets them on the ground. Zips it back up and walks toward the highway.

I look at the pile of stuff. Except for the candy bar, it surprises me. Kids usually steal beer, soda, chips. Not real food. I take a good look at her. She's small. Thin. Her legs and feet flame as sunburn-red as her face. Her hair is matted in the back. I wonder when she last combed it. When she last ate. "You shouldn't be hitchhiking!" I call after her.

She flips me off. Keeps walking.

I make a decision of my own. Grab the water, sandwich, and nuts. Shove the candy bar in my pocket. Trot after her. "Hey!"

She stops. Glances at what I'm carrying.

I hold it all out for her.

She meets my eyes. I think to see if I'm serious. She quickly opens her backpack. Shoves the sandwich and nuts inside. Holds on to the water. "What about the candy bar?"

"You don't need it."

She loops her backpack over her shoulder. Opens the water and takes a long drink.

"Why are you hitching?" I ask.

She shrugs.

"You really shouldn't. There are a lot of predators out there. Don't you watch the news?"

"I know what I'm doing. I can read people."

"Uh-huh. A trucker stops and offers you a lift. You can tell if he's going to rape you."

She takes another drink. Screws the top back on. "Yeah."

"That's not possible. You can't read what's in someone's head."

She gives me a long look. "Bye."

I watch as she walks away. At her red legs and feet. The hot sun beating down on her head. "Wait."

She turns. "What now?"

"I'm going to get you something. I'll be right back. Just hang on a second." I run into the store.

"Logan?" Grandma asks. "What's going on with that girl? Should I call the sheriff?"

"Everything's fine." I grab a bottle of sunscreen. One of the new baseball caps. I'm breathing heavy by the time I reach her. She's finishing the water. Tosses the empty bottle on the ground.

I hand her the cap and sunscreen. "Here."

She hesitates before taking them.

"What's your name?" I ask.

Pause. "Brooke."

"I'm Logan."

She slips the sunscreen into a side pocket of her backpack. "Where you headed?"

Another pause. Longer this time. "None of your business."

"I'm just curious how far you're going."

"Oklahoma City. To my grandmother."

"That's north. You should be on I-40, not I-10."

She looks at the cap she's still holding. "What's with all

the Geronimo crap? I saw like ten million billboards on the highway."

"He was a Native American."

"I know that."

"An Apache leader. There's a cave near the store. Legend says he hid there from the U.S. Army."

"Is that true?"

"I don't know. Could be. He did live around here back in the 1800s."

"So it's a gimmick to lure in tourists." She glances at the highway.

I can read people too. Side effect of spending so much time watching customers. She wants to get going, but she's dreading it. "You really should reconsider what you're doing. Want me to call someone for you?"

She narrows her eyes. "Why do you care?"

I shrug. "I'm just saying—"

She looks back at the cap. "Geronimo's Last Stand. What a bunch of crap. Can we make a trade? The candy bar for this lame cap?"

I clench my jaw. Shove my hand in my pocket. Hand it to her. It's soft and mushy from the heat.

She holds the cap out for me.

"Keep it," I say.

"I don't want it."

"Keep it anyway. Good luck reading people. I hope I

don't hear about you in the news. Another runaway girl found dead on the highway."

"Wow. That was nice. If you care so much, why don't you give me a ride?"

"I have to work."

"Right. Whatever."

"Yeah, whatever." I turn on my heels. Pick up the empty water bottle on my way back to the store.

I ring up everything I gave her. Pay with my own money.

"What was that about?" Grandma asks.

"I don't know." I really don't. "How's Dad?"

"Might be best if you take him home."

"You got things covered?"

Grandma smiles. "Yes, Logan. Our shifts are almost over anyway."

I go back to the staff room. Dad's curled up on the couch. I grab our lunch bags from the fridge. "Come on. Let's go."

He sits up. "I'm sorry."

"It's not your fault. Don't worry about it."

Chapter 3

I look for Brooke when we cross under the highway. Don't see her. Either someone picked her up already, or she walked out of sight.

I pull my pickup into the driveway. Our house is in the town of Ferris, Arizona. Population 864. Two miles from the store, opposite side of I-10. It's more a collection of houses than a real town. Although we have a post office. Tiny rural school. Cell tower. But that's more for highway drivers than us. Ferris used to be a lot bigger. Then the silver mine shut down in the 1960s. Grandpa says we're a town of scraggly mutts no one wants to adopt.

My grandparents live next door. Jethro barks in our yard. Barney barks in their yard.

Bark.

BARK!

Bark.

BARK!

Dad goes in the house ahead of me. I watch him. Make sure he doesn't trip on the crumbling front step. He disappears inside.

I get the mail from the box. Jethro's still barking, like he's birthing an elephant. "Calm down, doggie." I reach over the fence. Pet him. Did I feed him this morning?

I open the gate, then the back door. Throw the mail on the floor. Pour a bowl of dry food. Jethro tears into it the second I set it on the ground. Like he hasn't eaten in a week. "Faker," I tell him. I fill his water bowl from the hose.

I wonder where Brooke will find more water. She'll get dehydrated if she doesn't keep drinking. I wonder what she ate first from her stash. I'm guessing the candy bar. She seemed really desperate for it. She'll probably save the tuna sandwich for later. Snack on the nuts. I don't know why I think this. Or why I think about her at all. She's rude. Maybe a druggie. I'm guessing a lot of runaways are addicts. Definitely not my type. Not like Melody, whom I've had a crush on forever, even though she's my best friend's older sister. Even after Josh Becker got her pregnant. Then skipped out on her. Asshole.

I go inside. The screen door slams behind me. "Dad, you hungry?" I call.

"I could eat," he says from the living room.

I open the fridge. Find some of Grandma's leftover

chicken casserole. Carrots. Half an onion. Cheese slices. Milk. Hamburger patties in the freezer. I pull out four burgers and a bag of hash browns. Heat oil in a couple of frying pans.

Dad and I eat in front of the TV.

"Did you take your meds this morning?" I ask.

"Don't remember."

I shake my head. "Dad."

"I know! I'm sorry. I'll take them now."

"It's not like you can double up. That's not how it works."

"They don't do much good anyway."

"You have to give these new ones a chance. That's what the doc said. You remember *that*, don't you?"

He doesn't answer. Probably because he doesn't remember.

I carry our dishes to the kitchen.

"I'll clean up," he says.

"Okay. Thanks." I grab the mail off the floor. Head to my room and close the door. Flop onto my bed. I hate that Seth is at baseball camp. Hate these summer nights with nothing to do. My mind wanders back to Brooke, but that's a useless waste of brain space. I push her out of my head.

I look through the mail. Junk ads. Electric bill. Phone bill. A letter from Mom. I stare at her neat handwriting. The return address sticker with her Tucson address.

I open my desk drawer. Add it to the stack of other unopened letters and cards. Jump off my bed and go to the kitchen. Start the dishes.

"I said I'd do them," Dad says.

"I know. I'm antsy."

I finish up and step into the living room. Dad's watching TV. "Think I'll go out for a little while. Do you mind?"

"Where?" He gets a panicked look on his face.

"A drive. Nowhere special."

He clenches his hands. "I don't mind."

Of course he minds. But I can't stay in the house another second. "I'll call Grandma and Grandpa."

"You don't need to do that."

"I will anyway."

He shuts his eyes.

I use the kitchen phone. Grandpa answers.

"I'm going for a drive," I tell him. "I'll be back in an hour or two."

"Want one of us to come over?"

"No, he seems fine. I just wanted you to know. I'll call when I get back."

"I still wish you'd take us up on our offer."

"I don't need a vacation."

"Everyone needs a vacation now and then. Your mom—"

"Talk to you later." I hang up. Glance at the clock on

the stove. Five thirty. I grab my wallet. Phone. Keys. Open my underwear drawer. Take some of the cash I've been saving.

I pass Dad on the way out. "Go next door if you need anything, or call them. Okay?"

He doesn't respond.

"Dad?"

"I heard you."

"I'll be back before bedtime."

I pull the pickup out of the driveway. Jethro gazes at me forlornly through the fence. Shoot. Stupid dog. I don't spend enough time with him. I get out and open the gate. He hops in, tail wagging. Sits on the passenger seat and smiles.

"Let's go, doggie."

I pull onto the highway. Head east.

Chapter 4

It's about two hours since I saw Brooke at the store. I'm not much of a walker. Don't know how far a person can get in that amount of time. Especially if she stops to stick her thumb out.

I figure a trucker's picked her up by now. She's short. Cute, in an every-young-teenage-girl-is-cute kind of way. I don't know why, but I'm mostly worried about her skin. I got badly sunburned in fourth grade. Seth and I went to a swim party at Dimas Lake. Mom slathered me with sunscreen. Sent me on my way. But it must have been cheap stuff. Washed off while I swam. Next day I could barely move. I'd never felt anything so painful.

Brooke's skin looked like that. Red and raw.

I'm on the road about twenty minutes. Drive under the speed limit. Even so, she can't have walked this far. There's an interchange up ahead. I take a breath, hoping she really can read people. Hope she found someone nice to give her a lift. A family. Straight-A student on his way home from college. Woman with motherly instincts.

"Okay, doggie. Let's go home."

He yawns.

I pull off the freeway, and there she is. Walking up the off-ramp toward a truck stop. I idle on the shoulder in front of her. She walks by. Glances in at me.

"Hi, Brooke."

She stops. Narrows her eyes. "What do you want?"

"I thought about what you said. About giving you a lift."

She stares at me long and hard. Her face doesn't look any redder than before. I smell coconut-scented sunscreen. "I need to use the restroom," she says.

"Hop in and I'll drive you up there."

She thinks about it. Rounds the front of the pickup and gets in. Jethro hops onto the jumper seat, his usual spot. He knows he's had it good until now.

I drive. Park in front of the store. "Better not shoplift," I warn her. "These are the big boys. They have cameras and a security detail. They won't hesitate turning you in."

She glares at me. Slams the door and goes inside.

"Was it something I said?" I ask Jethro.

He watches the store, like he's waiting for her.

She comes back a few minutes later. Gets in but leaves the door open. "So how far can you drive me?"

"San Bueno. It's just the other side of the border in New Mexico, about an hour from here. Then I need to get home."

She looks over at all of the parked semi trucks.

"Most of those drivers are eating dinner," I tell her. "Or using the pay showers. Some are bedding down in their trucks for the night."

"But they can take me a lot farther."

"Probably."

She sighs.

"There's a Greyhound stop in San Bueno," I say.

"I don't have money for a bus."

I act like I'm thinking about it. But the truth is I decided before I left home. "I'll buy you a ticket."

She stares at me. "Why would you do that?"

"Because I work. Save my money. Don't have anything to spend it on." Then I add, "I don't want anything in exchange, if that's what you're thinking."

She sits there. Looks out at the trucks. "Okay." She closes the door.

I start the engine.

"I forgot your name," she says.

"Logan." I back out of the parking lot. Head east on the highway.

Brooke fiddles with the radio. The only stations with reception are country western. She turns it off.

"Hey, leave it on."

"You like that crap?"

"Something's not crap just because you don't like it."

She turns the radio back on. Looks over her shoulder at Jethro and cringes. "Your dog stinks."

"Jethro's mostly an outdoor dog. Doesn't get washed very often."

"Jethro. That's a redneck name. Are you guys rednecks?" She pats his head. He licks her fingers. "Ew." She wipes them on her shorts.

"No, we're not rednecks. You haven't spent much time around dogs, have you?"

"My dad's allergic."

"He's allergic to dogs?"

"Animal dander."

"Wow. I didn't know that was a thing."

"It is. Big-time. A bunch of my friends are too."

"Is that why you're running away from home? You want a pet and can't have one?"

She squints at me.

"I'm kidding."

"You're prying. Who says I'm running away?"

"Well, you are, aren't you?"

She folds her arms over her chest. Stares out the passenger window.

"It's a big decision to leave home," I say. "Especially the way you're doing it."

"You sound like a therapist."

"I don't know what a therapist sounds like."

"They act like they care. But they don't. Not really. They just want you to open up and spill your guts. So they feel good about themselves. Like they've accomplished something."

"I'm not like that."

She shrugs. Unzips her backpack and pulls out a cell phone. Presses a button. Throws it back.

"Dead battery?"

She nods.

"You can use mine."

She crosses her arms again. Turns her head. Presses her forehead against the window.

The sun is getting low. The landscape is flat and barren. Nothing to look at except a dust devil. A long freight train in the distance is keeping pace with us.

"What was with that guy in your store?" she asks. "The one who freaked out when the car backfired?"

"That's my dad."

"Really? What's wrong with him?"

"He was in an accident four years ago. Got a concussion. His brain is damaged. He has anxiety, panic attacks, memory problems. I take care of him."

"Where's your mom?"

I grip the steering wheel. "Now who's prying?"

"I don't care. You don't have to tell me."

Jethro snakes his nose between the seats. Rests his chin on my thigh. I pet him. "How about I tell you about my mom and you tell me about yours?"

"How about we don't."

"My mom left us three years ago," I start. "Eight months after Dad's accident. She couldn't put up with him. Or where we lived. Or me."

"Why? What's wrong with you?"

"I don't know. There must be something. She gave up on us."

"That sucks."

I look over at her. "Your turn."

She fidgets. Winces.

"Your sunburn hurt?"

"Yeah."

"It will be worse tomorrow."

"Great. Good to know. So, my mom is a drunk. And my dad abused me."

"Abused you? How?"

"Does it matter? He abused me." She tucks her feet under her. Curls into a ball.

"Sorry," I say. "Didn't mean to upset you."

"Can we shut up now? I want to sleep." She leans her head against the window.

I watch her for a moment. Reach behind the seat and grab the hoodie I always keep back there. "Here."

She opens her eyes. Glares at the sweatshirt. "I'm not cold."

"Pillow."

She balls it up. Sticks it under her head.

Chapter 5

Brooke sleeps the rest of the way to San Bueno. Or at least she pretends to. I pull into town. The bus station is at the Stop 'n' Save on Main Street. I've never taken a bus from here or anywhere. But I work on this highway, which means I answer a lot of questions. Learn about transportation options.

I park next to the store. It's almost seven thirty. The sun is sinking below the horizon. Jethro gets to his feet. Wags his tail.

"We're here," I tell both of them.

Brooke raises her head. Looks around. "A convenience store?" She stretches her legs.

"And bus stop. They sell tickets inside." I open my door.

"Where are you going?"

"To buy your ticket."

"I can do it. I know you need to get home."

"Except I don't know how much it costs. So I don't know how much to give you."

She sighs. "Fine." She gets out. Drags her backpack with her. "Bye, Jethro." She slams the door.

The cashier eyes us as we enter. I know that look. He's guessing our threat level. If the two of us came into my store, I'd rate us a seven out of ten. Strangers. Teens. At night. Good chance one of us might cause a distraction while the other nabs something. He glances outside, wondering if we have accomplices.

"I'd like a bus ticket," I say.

His shoulders drop. Gaze softens. I guess people who buy bus tickets aren't troublemakers. "Where to?" he asks.

"Oklahoma City."

He opens a laptop and taps on it. "When?"

"Soonest you got."

"The next eastbound bus comes through at eight fifty. Fourteen-hour ride. One transfer. Gets to the main station in Oklahoma City at eleven fifteen tomorrow. One hundred ninety-eight dollars."

That's a lot of money. But I'm not going to back out now. "Okay." I count out ten twenties.

The cashier looks out into the store. "Hey, you," he calls. "Girl with the backpack. Either you or your backpack needs to stay up here where I can watch you."

Brooke's in the candy aisle. She rolls her eyes. "I'm not going to steal anything."

"Regardless." He crooks his finger.

She slowly steps up to the counter. "Fourteen hours is a long time on a bus."

"They're comfortable seats," he says. "You can sleep most of the way."

She frowns. Bites her bottom lip.

"Do you still have that tuna sandwich?" I ask.

She nods. A printer churns behind the counter. I give her a twenty. "Use this for snacks and breakfast." I pull out my phone. "Call your grandma. Tell her you're coming."

Brooke hesitates. Carries the phone outside. The door closes behind her.

The ticket finishes printing. The cashier slides it across the counter. "She should be out front fifteen minutes before departure. We're a small stop. The driver doesn't wait long."

"Gotcha. Thanks." I take the ticket and leave the store. The sky is darker now. Temp a little cooler, but still hot. I look around for Brooke. Don't see her. "Brooke?"

She steps around the side of the building, gripping the phone.

"Everything okay?" I ask.

"Yeah." She's biting her lip again.

"Get in touch with your grandma?"

She nods.

"And she can pick you up tomorrow?"

"God, you're worse than my mother!"

"Okay, relax. I'm invested in you now. I just want to make sure you'll be okay." I give her the bus ticket.

She stares at it. Turns it over.

"I hope everything works out." I'm not sure what else to say. So I just say, "See ya."

"Right. See ya."

I walk to the pickup and open the door. I forgot to mention about not being late. I turn to tell her, but she's gone. "Brooke?"

No sign of her. I push down the urge to search. Figure she went back into the store to buy water or something. If I don't hurry, I'll miss Dad's bedtime. He'll fall asleep on the couch. Wake up wondering where he is. Where I am. Mess up his routine. He needs his routine.

I call Grandma and Grandpa just to be safe.

Grandpa answers with, "Everything okay, Logan?"

"Yeah. I'm in San Bueno. Drove farther than I should have. Can you—"

"Sure. I'll head over there right now."

"I should be home before his bedtime. But just in case, I put his pj's in the hamper this morning. He'll need clean ones. And he needs to take his meds—"

"I've got it. Don't worry. Just drive carefully."

"Make sure he uses the toothpaste for sensitive teeth. The regular is mine—"

"Logan? I've got it. Goodbye." He hangs up.

I end the call. Close the pickup door. Pat the passenger seat. "Come on, doggie."

Jethro scrambles up front.

I start the engine. Pull out of the parking lot.

Jethro whines and squirms.

"Need to pee?"

He yips.

I park at the edge of the Stop 'n' Save next to a used car lot. I clip on the leash I keep in the glove box. Walk him along the dirt shoulder.

Someone comes out of the store. It's Brooke. She's carrying a bulging plastic bag. She stops. Looks over to where I'd parked the pickup before. Then walks to the sidewalk. Turns away from Jethro and me. Toward the highway.

What the hell?

"Hey!" I call.

She looks over her shoulder. Her body sags at the sight of me.

I trot over with Jethro. "Where are you going?"

She shrugs. "Nowhere. For a walk."

"The bus will be here soon."

"I'll be back in time."

I glance at the bag she's carrying. I know how much

twenty dollars buys. Not as much as what's in that bag. "What did you buy?"

"Snacks, like you said."

I pull the bag out of her hand.

"Hey!" she says, grabbing for it.

I swing it out of reach and look inside. Several caffeine drinks. A pile of candy bars. Bags of chips. Even a T-shirt.

She takes it back from me.

"Show me the bus ticket," I say.

"Why?"

"Show me the bus ticket!"

She shakes her head.

I stick my hand out. "Then give me the rest of the money."

"What money?"

"The money you got for cashing in the ticket."

She stares at me. Takes a deep breath and reaches into her pocket. Pulls out some bills and hands them to me.

"Eighty dollars?" I ask.

"There was a cancellation fee."

I clench my jaw. Try not to blow up. "So what's your plan? Going back to the highway? Hitching again?"

"Maybe."

"Do you know how dangerous that is at night?"

"I know what I'm doing."

"Because you can *read* people? That is the stupidest thing I've ever heard. Do you have a death wish?"

She shrugs.

"I can't let you do this."

"It's a free country. I can do what I want." Then she says, "I really don't get why you give a crap."

I think about it. "Say I drive off right now. And something terrible happens to you when I could have helped but didn't. I couldn't live with that."

"You are so weird."

"It's what people do. They help each other."

"Not on my planet."

"Well, you're on my planet now."

Chapter 6

Come on," I tell Brooke. I head with Jethro back toward the Stop 'n' Save.

"Where are you going?"

"To buy you a bus ticket to Oklahoma City. Then I'm going to wait with you until it gets here."

She trots next to me. "I don't believe this."

We reach the store. I hand her Jethro's leash. "Stay here. I'll be right back."

"What do I do with your dog?"

"Nothing. Just stand there."

I glance at her when I get in line at the counter. She's leaning against a DVD vending machine.

The clerk finishes with the customer ahead of me. "I want that bus ticket to Oklahoma City." I set two hundred dollars in front of him.

He smirks. "Glad you caught her. I knew something was fishy. Is she your sister? A cousin?"

"No."

He gives me a long look. I'm not going to explain.

He refunds the penalty, thankfully. But it should be forty more than what Brooke gave me. She must have kept it. I pocket the bus ticket. Get a black coffee and three waters. Pay for them and leave.

Jethro's leash is tied to a bike rack.

Brooke is gone.

"Damn it."

Jethro gazes up at me.

"Where did she go?"

He wags his tail.

I wasn't in there more than ten minutes. Fifteen at the most. She can't have gone far. I jump in the pickup with Jethro. Drive down Main Street. Don't see her on the sidewalk. The highway is close. I suppose she might have gotten that far.

I pull onto the onramp. Have to speed up to avoid a big rig. Did I miss her? I look in the rearview mirror. Don't see a thing. It's too dark. Shoot! There won't be another exit for twenty miles. I pound the steering wheel. There's a crossing road up ahead. It's for emergency vehicles only. I can get a huge fine if I use it.

I slam on the breaks. Make a sharp turn onto the sandy road. Dirt flies from my tires. In seconds I'm driving west. I check the mirror for flashing lights. Then I search the other shoulder for Brooke.

Did she get a ride already? I wasn't joking when I told her it's more dangerous at night. The worst slimeballs slither in darkness.

I take the exit into San Bueno. No one's behind me, so I drive slowly. Search both sides of Main Street. I check the pickup's clock. It's close to eight thirty. Is it possible she's at the Stop 'n' Save? Maybe she took a leak when I was in the store. Slipped by me.

I'm such an idiot.

The tires squeal as I pull a U-turn at the next intersection. I race back to the Stop 'n' Save. She's not outside. I park and run into the store. "Brooke?" I call.

"Not here," the cashier says from behind the counter.

"Has she been in here at all since I left?"

"Nope."

I comb my fingers through my hair. Try to think what to do.

"It's none of my business," he says. "But are you sending her to rehab?"

"What?"

"Happened to a niece of mine. Family had a heck of a time getting her to go. She kept running away."

"She's going to her grandmother's."

He snickers. "Must hate her grandmother something fierce."

"Of course she doesn't."

But I don't know, do I? Maybe she does hate her grand-mother. But why would she run away to a place she doesn't want to be? And why would she rather hitchhike than take a bus? The only thing that makes sense is the shoplifting. And the money she stole. She's broke.

"Where did your niece run off to?" I ask, desperate for clues.

"To her friends. Anywhere she could get her hands on drugs. There's a local bar. You might want to check it out."

"She's too young for a bar."

He shrugs. "Not for this place. It's the Rockin' Pony. Two blocks south."

I don't thank him because I hate what he thinks about her. I charge out of the store. Then run back in. Grab a large empty coffee cup. Don't look at the cashier as I leave.

I drive two blocks south. The whole time I'm wondering why I'm bothering with this girl. She's a thief. Hasn't thanked me once. She may be a drug addict on top of it.

I guess the reason is exactly what I told her. I can help, so what would it say about me if I didn't? This is just something I need to do.

I pass the Rockin' Pony on the right. Pull over. Open the window a crack for Jethro. Lock the pickup's doors.

The bar's harsh smell hits me when I open the door. Stale beer. Cigarette smoke. Urine. It's not possible she's here. Then I hear a girl's laughter. I've never heard Brooke laugh before. I wouldn't know her laugh from a hyena's. But my gut tells me it's her.

I pass the crowded bar. Head to the back. There are a couple of pool tables. Brooke is holding a cue. Leaning over a table and lining up a shot. She's playing with some guy. Two men are using the other table.

"Brooke?" I say.

She looks up at me. "Oh my God. Really?"

"You can still make the bus, but you'll need to hurry."

She levels her eyes down the cue again. Shoots. The ball goes wide of the pocket. She straightens. "Thanks. You messed up my concentration."

"So, are you coming?"

"No."

I tap the edge of a table. "I wish you would. You shouldn't be in here."

"I wish you'd leave me alone. Stop acting like you own me."

The guy she's playing with steps up next to her. Maybe mid-twenties. Taller and beefier than me. "Is this guy bothering you?" he asks.

"Yeah, he is."

The guy looks at me. "You should go." He rests his hand on the small of Brook's back. Slides it down to her butt and squeezes.

Brooke quickly moves away from him. Stands with

her back against the wall. Takes a long drink from a bottle of beer.

"She's underage," I say.

He angles his cue across his chest. "Well, aren't you a Boy Scout? Seems like she can take care of herself."

This is getting hairy. More than I bargained for. Maybe she *can* take care of herself. Maybe this really is none of my business. If she's hell-bent on self-destruction, maybe I should let her. I look at Brooke for a sign. If this is really what she wants.

She stares at her beer. Shifts her feet. Tucks a strand of hair behind her ear. She's nervous. Scared. I think his hand on her butt shook her up. That bad-girl thing? I'm pretty sure it's an act.

I'm not leaving her here.

Chapter 7

Brooke?" I say to her. "Come on."

She stands there, frozen. Finally sets down her beer. Picks up her backpack and shopping bag. Steps toward me.

"Hey, wait a minute!" The guy grips her arm as she passes. "We were having a nice game. I thought you were having fun."

"Let me go," she murmurs.

"Let her go." I stand tall. Stare him in the eyes. Try not to shake. If it comes to a fight, he'll kill me.

The guy looks from her, to me, and back again. Pushes her away. "Jail bait. I don't need the hassle."

I grip her hand. Pull her out of the bar.

She shakes my hand off when we're outside.

I point up the street. "The pickup's over there."

She trots to the pickup. Jumps in when I unlock it. Jethro moves to the back.

I start the engine. Brooke buries her face in her hands.

Is she crying? I'm not sure. Jethro rests his chin on her thigh.

I drive to the Stop 'n' Save. The bus is there, idling in the parking lot. I pull the ticket from my pocket.

She looks at it. Takes it. Her cheeks glisten with tears.

"You'd better hurry," I tell her. "It won't wait long."

She reaches for the door handle. "Then I guess I'd better go." Her voice is flat. Sad. Exhausted.

I grab an old receipt. Write my phone number on it. Hand it to her. "Call me if you want to talk."

She opens the door. Grabs her stuff. Gets out. Takes a few steps.

I sigh. "Brooke?"

She looks back at me. "What?"

"Hold on a second."

"You said I needed to hurry."

I pull out my phone. Decide whom to call first. Grandpa may still be at Dad's. Two birds with one stone. I call my home number.

Grandpa answers with, "Hey, Logan. What's up?"

"I have a favor to ask. I don't exactly feel like coming home. I was thinking of a road trip. I've got cash with me. You've been telling me to take a vacation."

"Well, yeah. But a little warning would be nice. We need to get someone to cover for you at the store."

"Oh, right. Sorry. I'll head back right now."

"Not so fast! Jeepers. Give me a second to think about it. How long are we talking? Days? Weeks?"

"A couple of days."

"Okay. Bev has been wanting extra work. She can pull a double. I think Alex is available. We'll work it out."

"But there's Dad," I think aloud. "Maybe I shouldn't do this."

"Logan. He may be your father, but he's our son. We'll take good care of him."

"I should talk to him."

"He's already in bed. I was just leaving. I'll tell him in the morning."

"But what if he wakes up in the night? And I'm not there?"

"I'll leave him a note."

"I don't want him to freak out."

"None of us want that. But there's not much you can do to prevent it. Unless you can get inside his brain and rewire it. Can you do that?"

"No."

"Right. Didn't think so. So where are you going?"

"Um … I'm not sure yet. East."

"San Antonio's nice. You can visit the Alamo."

"Maybe I will."

"Enjoy yourself."

"Okay, Grandpa. Thanks. I've got Jethro, by the way."

I end the call. Look over at Brooke. She's back in the pickup. Petting my dog.

"Looks like I'm driving you to Oklahoma City."

She nods. "The bus already left."

Sure enough. Except for us, the parking lot is empty.

She closes the door. Picks up my hoodie off the floor. Wads it up. Stuffs it under her head.

"I have to buy gas," I say. "I need the money you didn't return."

She sighs. Rummages inside her backpack. Pulls out two twenties and hands them to me.

"Do you have a drug problem?" I ask.

"What?"

"Is that why you were at that bar? Looking for drugs?"

"Hey." She glares at me. "I didn't ask you to buy me a bus ticket. Or give me a ride. Or save me from that idiot. All of this is your choice. I don't owe you any explanation."

"All right. I was just …" I shake my head. "Never mind."

I pull up to a gas pump. Step inside the store.

"Forty dollars on pump three," I tell the same cashier.

He glances outside at my pickup. "So you found her. Too bad you wasted all that money on a ticket."

I leave without comment.

I pump gas. Clean the windshield. Pour water into the Styrofoam cup I took earlier. Hold it while Jethro licks sloppily.

"Yuck," Brooke says.

I get in. Point at the water bottle in the cup holder closest to her. "That's yours if you want it." I buckle my seat belt. "Buckle up," I tell her.

"Okay, Dad. Whatever you say, Dad."

I take a sip of coffee. It's cold. I drink half of it anyway. Would prefer to not see that cashier ever again.

Brooke takes something from her backpack as I pull onto the highway. I hear plastic wrap and smell tuna. Hard to believe she took that sandwich from my store earlier today.

She hands me half. I take it. The bread is soggy. It's probably not fit to eat at this point. But it tastes surprisingly good.

"Aren't you going to say thank you?" she says.

"I bought it."

"Oh. So I guess I should thank you." She tosses the empty container into her plastic bag. Curls into her seat. Uses my sweatshirt as a pillow.

I wait for a thank you that doesn't come. Turn on the radio.

The highway stretches into darkness.

Chapter 8

Brooke's left foot jiggles over the edge of the passenger seat. She snores lightly and mumbles in her sleep.

It's one thirty. I've been driving for four hours. Four hours of second-guessing myself, wondering again what in the hell I'm doing. Wasting vacation days on this juvenile delinquent. I glance at her bare legs. Her sunburn is turning brown already. She must be one of those lucky people who tan instead of blister. Her skin is really smooth. Soft. I look at her face. She seems even younger when she sleeps.

A semi passes. A whoosh of air rocks the pickup. I breathe in and focus on the road. The yellow divider line starts playing tricks on my brain. Is the pickup moving? Or are we standing still and the road's moving?

I blink a few times. Need more coffee. Or sleep. Brooke's bag is full of caffeine drinks. But that would require leaning over and taking my eyes off the road. I could pull over and stop. But don't want to wake her.

I turn up the radio slightly. Tap the steering wheel.

We're suddenly bouncing across dirt.

A semi blasts its horn.

Brooke screams.

Jethro barks.

I slam on the brakes. Wrestle with the steering wheel. Try to keep from fishtailing. Bring the pickup to a stop on the right shoulder. My heart is hammering.

"What happened?" Brooke's voice shakes.

I take a couple of deep breaths before I try to answer. "I went to sleep. I've been up over twenty hours. It's still a long way to Oklahoma City. I won't make it."

"What do you mean?"

"I mean I need to sleep."

"Where? Here?"

"At a motel."

"Are you kidding me?"

I look over my left shoulder. Speed up and pull the pickup back onto the highway.

She takes a can from her shopping bag. "Drink this."

"That won't do me any good. Not at this point."

"Do you have enough money for two rooms?"

"I don't think so," I say.

"I'm not staying in a motel room with you."

"Then you can sleep in the pickup with Jethro."

She crosses her arms. Stares out the window. "Where are we?"

"East of Albuquerque. Don't know where exactly."

"We're still in New Mexico?" she asks.

"Had to go north before we could head east again."

The driving mishap wakes me up a little. Enough to drive another ten miles to a chain motel just off the highway.

I leave Brooke in the pickup. Go to the empty lobby. Press my thumb on the night buzzer. It takes a while to rouse a clerk from the back. I pay cash for a room with two double beds. At least it's cheap. Which is good, because I'll need another motel on the way back. Plus gas and food.

"Room 213. Checkout is eleven," the young woman says. She can't be much older than me. "Breakfast is six to ten."

"Thanks."

I park the pickup closer to room 213. "It's got two beds," I tell Brooke. "I'm going to walk Jethro. You can join me in the room or not. I'm too tired to argue." I give her a key card.

She sits there while I leash my dog. I take him for a pee. I'll need to find him something to eat in the morning. I'll figure it out later.

I let him back in the pickup. Open the window a couple of inches. Say, "Be good, doggie." Then I drag myself upstairs. Fall on the farthest bed. Don't bother undressing or getting under the covers.

I'm barely aware of the door opening and then closing. A light turning on. The bathroom door opening. Closing. The room turning dark again.

଼

I wake up from a dream. Tires sliding across dirt. A terrified scream. Only it's Mom screaming, not Brooke.

I sit up. Slivers of sunlight filter through the blinds. A form curls under a blanket on the other bed. Brooke's dark hair peaks out the top. It just now occurs to me. I'm in a motel room with a girl.

A motel room.

With a girl.

My mind goes straight to places it shouldn't. Like crawling under those covers with her. And more. Crap! That's not why I'm helping her. I cannot think like this. But now the thought is lodged in my head. I can't get rid of it.

I go to the bathroom. Take a long shower. Wash my hair with the little bottle of motel shampoo. Leave enough for Brooke. Pull on my dirty clothes. They feel gross. My mouth is gross too. I swish some water and spit it out, but it doesn't help.

I step out of the bathroom. Brooke is sitting on the side of her bed, her back to me. Her head lowered.

"Good morning," I say.

She sits up in a hurry. Quickly shoves something under her blanket.

"What was that?" I ask.

"What?"

"Whatever it is you just hid in your bed."

"I don't know what you're talking about."

"Yes you do." I can't shake the idea of her doing drugs. I know it's none of my business, but I charge over there. Flip the blanket back. Something flies and lands on the floor.

I pick it up.

A razor blade?

She steps over to me. Holds out her hand.

I give it to her. Narrow my eyes.

"It's nothing," she says. She opens a small plastic box. Slips the blade inside. Turns away from me. But I can see her in the mirror on the wall. She lifts her T-shirt. There's a fresh cut about two-inches long next to her navel. She dabs the blood with a tissue. Her stomach is striped with scars.

"Did you just *cut* yourself?" I ask in disbelief. My insides twist. I think I'm going to be sick.

Chapter 9

Brooke notices me in the mirror. Quickly lowers her shirt. "Leave me alone."

"How can you do that?"

Her cheeks redden beneath her tanning face. She doesn't answer.

Everything else I can handle. Her being a runaway. Maybe a druggie. But this? It's crazy. Which means she's definitely crazy. Which makes me want to jump in my pickup. Drive back to Ferris. Forget about her.

Then she says softly, "It makes me feel better."

"Hurting yourself makes you feel better? I don't get it."

"Of course you don't. Nobody does. Except other people like me."

"Well … I'd like to understand."

"Really?" she says sarcastically. "Really and truly?"

I don't know what to say. Mostly I don't want to know.

"I can see it in your face," she says. "I gross you out. You should leave. Go. I'll be fine."

"But—"

"I'm not going to my grandmother's anyway. When you stopped me yesterday, I was on my way to see my boyfriend. He lives in New Orleans. That's why I was on I-10, not I-40. Now I'm totally out of my way. So thank you very much, Logan."

I stare at her in complete disbelief. "I drove all this way. Wasted money on a bus ticket. Almost got us killed. To take you someplace you don't want to go? Why didn't you tell me sooner? Why did you lie?"

"I didn't lie about my grandmother. She does live in Oklahoma City. I lied about where I was going because I was afraid you were about to turn me in for shoplifting." She looks me in the eyes. "Which sounds more sympathetic? Hitching to my grandma, or hitching to my boyfriend?"

I think about it. "I get your point. But you could have said something when we got to San Bueno." I laugh and shake my head. "You needed the money. From the bus ticket."

She shrugs.

"Then why did you let me drive you here?"

"Because you were being really pushy."

"No, it was the guy in the bar. He freaked you out. You've never hitchhiked before, have you? And you're not good at reading people. This whole thing terrifies you."

"Have a nice life." She walks to the bathroom. Slams the door.

Now what? Now nothing. I'm going home. Or maybe to San Antonio, like Grandpa suggested. I glance at the clock. Nine fifty-five. I grab my keys. Run down to the lounge.

A worker is clearing the breakfast buffet.

I grab two yogurts. A plastic spoon. Two hardboiled eggs. Muffins. Banana and apple. Coffee. Carry everything back to the pickup. Set it on the hood.

Jethro yips. Scratches at the window. It's covered with his slobber.

I open the door a crack. "Hey, doggie. Sorry I kept you waiting." I reach in and attach the leash to his collar. Let him out. He runs to the nearest bush. Pees. Then squats and poops. I hope no one's watching. I don't have anything to pick it up with.

I take him back to the pickup. Give him water. Feed him two eggs. He swallows them whole. Gazes at me, asking for more.

I pile the rest of the food on the dashboard. He eyes the muffins.

"That's not good dog food." He licks his lips. "Okay, just this once." I give him a muffin while I dig into a yogurt.

A hotel door slams. Brooke is lugging her backpack and plastic bag down the stairs. She's wearing her flip-flops.

Same shorts as yesterday. Her hair is wet. She's wearing her new shirt, the one she bought yesterday with my money. It's yellow. Butterflies on the front. *New Mexico* written across the bottom.

She doesn't look at me as she passes the pickup. Walks straight for the lounge.

I start the pickup. Pull up beside her and roll down the passenger window. "If you're looking for breakfast, you're too late." I hold a yogurt out for her.

She tries the door. It rattles. Locked. She looks at the yogurt. "Do you have a spoon?"

"Not a clean one. But I'm done with mine."

She eyes the dirty spoon with disgust. But takes it along with the yogurt.

"I was just thinking," I say. "We're only six hours from Oklahoma City. Do you have any interest in seeing your grandmother?"

She pulls the foil off the yogurt. Licks it. Looks out at the highway for a while. Her shoulders rise and fall with a deep breath. She rounds the front of the pickup.

"Go in the back, Jethro," I say. "We have company."

Brooke gets in. Settles her backpack and shopping bag on the floor. Buckles her seat belt. Grabs a muffin from the dashboard.

I drive to the onramp. Pull onto the highway. Head east.

Brooke turns and looks at Jethro. "Your truck stinks like your dog now."

"Haven't exactly had a chance to wash him."

We drive quietly for a while. "So is that why you know so much about therapists?' I ask.

"What?"

"You know … what you were doing in the motel room."

She doesn't answer.

"With the razor," I add.

"Yeah, I get it!" She slips off her flip-flops. Raises her feet onto the dashboard. "That and other things. So can I ask you a question?"

I shrug.

"Did you want to have sex with me in the motel room?"

My cheeks burn. "No."

"Why not? Do you think I'm ugly?"

"You're not ugly."

"Are you gay? That would explain a lot."

"Explain what?" I glare at her.

She studies me, like she's trying to see inside my head. "I had this gay friend in junior high. He treated me like his sister. Real protective."

"I'm not gay. You're too young. And I hardly know you. It wouldn't be right. That's why I didn't try anything."

"So you did want to."

I roll my eyes. "Criminy."

She laughs. "*Criminy*. Do people really say that? I bet you're a virgin."

God, I hate this conversation. I feel like dropping her off right here.

"You're fidgeting," she's says. "You *are* a virgin, aren't you? How old are you?"

"How old are you?"

"Sixteen."

"Right. You're fourteen. Fifteen at the most."

She's quiet a moment. "At least I'm not a virgin."

"And you're proud of that?"

She shrugs. Lowers her feet. Grabs a caffeine drink out of her bag. Drinks half of it. "Oh. Do you want one?"

The hotel coffee tastes like crap. "Yeah. Especially since I paid for everything in that bag. Including the shirt you're wearing."

She pops open a can. Hands it to me. "The shirt's not really my style. Yellow. Butterflies."

"Didn't think so."

"Better than wearing dirty clothes."

"You must have left home in a hurry."

She stares out the passenger window again. I guess we're back to not talking.

Chapter 10

We make a pit stop in Texas near the Oklahoma border. Brooke comes into the store with me. I get in line to pay for gas while trying to keep an eye on her. I don't know what all of her issues are. One could be shoplifting. I hear people do it for the heck of it. Like an addiction.

She joins me in line with a carton of gooey nachos.

"Those are hard to eat while I'm driving," I say.

"They're not for you."

"Wow! Thanks. Could you maybe grab me an egg salad sandwich? Three waters?"

She sighs and hands me the nachos. Heads to the cooler.

I pay for the gas and food. Brooke sits in the pickup and eats while I pump gas. She licks melted cheese off her fingers. Her selfishness amazes me. At home we're always helping each other. I could never just watch while someone else does all the work. Or take something without saying thank you.

I tap on the driver's window. "Hey. Think you could wash the windshield?"

She rolls her eyes. Gets slowly out of the pickup.

The pump clicks off. I take Jethro for a walk. Pour him some water. Brooke is still washing the windshield when we return. Or trying to. She's short and it's a long reach. I can't help smiling. It's kind of cute.

She gets back in the pickup and picks up her nachos. There are streaks of dirt on the glass.

"I take it you haven't done a lot of manual labor."

She shrugs.

I pull out my cell phone. Set it on the console. "We're a couple hours from Oklahoma City. Might want to call your grandmother, give her a little warning. Do you know how to get to her house?"

"Yeah. I've been there a bunch of times." She takes the phone. Taps in a number. A moment later, she says, "Hi, Gram. I'm fine … She did? Yeah, well, I got a ride." She glances at me. "I'm really okay. I'll be there in a couple of hours … Right. Bye." She hands the phone back to me.

"Sounds like she knows you ran away."

"My mom called. Warned her I might come this way. Can we go now?"

"Seat belt."

She sighs. Buckles up.

I get the pickup back onto the highway. She plays with

the radio. There's more reception now. She finds a pop station and leaves it there.

"When's the last time you saw your grandmother?" I ask.

She takes the apple from the dashboard. Bites into it. "Two years exactly. I used to visit her every summer."

"Why did you stop?"

"It got boring. I had other things to do."

"Do you miss her?"

She stretches her feet out. Takes another bite of apple. "I guess. Yeah."

"I live next door to my grandma and grandpa," I say. "Work with them. See them almost every day. They're really important to me."

"What about *your* mom? When's the last time you saw her?"

"The day she left."

"That would be okay with me. To never see my mom again."

"Really? Why?"

She sets the partly eaten apple back on the dashboard. "Because she's always telling me what to do. She hates my friends. Especially my boyfriend. Hates my clothes. My hair. Hates that I'm getting straight Cs. Hates that I want to be a musician. She doesn't get me at all."

"She gets you enough to know you might visit your grandmother. Sounds to me like she worries. Like she just wants what's best for you."

Brooke glares at me. "You don't know anything."

"I'm just giving you my point of view. From an outsider's perspective."

"What about your mom? Does she worry about you? Does she want what's best for you?"

"My situation's different. She ran away from me. Not the other way around."

"But you haven't seen her in the last three years, right? Did you ever get her side of the story? Do you know for a fact she doesn't care about you?"

I flash on all of Mom's unopened letters.

"That's just my point of view," Brooke adds. "You know, from an outsider's perspective."

"Fine. I get it. Maybe we shouldn't talk about our families."

She crosses her arms over her chest. "Maybe we shouldn't."

Jethro presses his nose against my arm. I pet him. "So, your boyfriend. Is he a safe topic?"

She smirks.

"What's his name?"

"Anthrax."

"Like the poison?"

"That's his stage name. He's a drummer with the Bashing Pancakes. We met at a concert last March. My friends and I went backstage."

"Then what? You started dating?"

"Sort of. I'd meet him at his gigs. You know … hang out."

"Does he know you were planning to see him?"

"Sure. I texted. Left a few messages."

"Maybe he's not even in New Orleans. Did you think about that?"

"He is. I know his schedule. They aren't going on the road again until the end of July."

I take a bite from the uneaten side of the apple. Throw the rest away. "Are the Bashing Pancakes famous?"

"Not yet. But they will be once I'm singing vocals. That's one reason I'm going out there, to audition. Talk him into it."

"I see."

"*I see.* You sound like my dad. Like you don't believe me."

"I believe you. I don't know anything about the music business. I only know what goes on in a highway convenience store."

"And that's what you're going to do for the rest of your life? Clean bathrooms? Sell stuff to grumpy truck drivers? Pick up teenage hitchhikers?"

"There are a lot worse ways to spend a life."

"God, that is so pathetic."

I stare at her. "There's nothing wrong with having a good job. Or helping my family."

"Dude, whatever you say."

We drive quietly for over an hour. Which is good. Talking to her makes me twitchy.

We pass under a mileage sign. Forty miles to Oklahoma City.

Ten miles later Brooke starts squirming. She changes the radio station. Downs a caffeine drink in a couple of swallows. Pulls her backpack onto her lap. Rummages around. Throws it on the floor.

"What's wrong?" I ask.

"I need a restroom."

"We're almost there. Can you hold it a few more miles?"

"I need a restroom. Now!"

Chapter 11

I take the next off-ramp. See a McDonald's on the right. Brooke is out of the pickup before I stop. She takes her backpack with her.

Okay.

"Want a burger?" I ask Jethro. "Need to pee?"

He barely raises his head from his paws. Guess I woke him up.

I go inside. Buy a Coke and fries.

Brooke returns to the pickup a little after me. Tosses her backpack on the floor. Buckles her seatbelt without being asked. I hold out the carton of fries.

She takes a few. "Thanks."

I gape at her.

"What?" she says.

"Of all the things you could thank me for, you choose french fries."

She sticks the fries back in the carton. "Never mind, I'm not hungry. Let's go."

"Yes, ma'am."

She pulls her feet up under her. Wraps her arms around her stomach. Like she's trying to make herself small.

I start the engine. Get back on the highway.

"I think it's pretty brave what you're doing," I say. "Must be kind of stressful seeing your grandmother after so long."

She doesn't say anything. I glance over. She's holding her arm away from her stomach and staring down at herself. "Crap," she says.

"What?"

She quickly unzips her backpack. Pulls out that little plastic box, the one with the razor blade.

"Whoa. Wait a minute."

"Shut up, okay?" She takes something out of the box. I get a glimpse of her shirt. There's blood on it.

Traffic is heavy. Four lanes of it. And I'm in the left. I watch behind me. Pull over to the right. Stop on the shoulder. Turn on the hazard lights. Jethro sits up. Whines.

Brooke has pulled her shirt up. She's pressing something against her stomach. It looks like gauze, and it's red with blood.

"What did you do?"

"What do you think I did?" Her eyes fill with tears. She looks down at herself. "Crap."

I reach for the ignition. "I'll find a hospital."

"No! I just need a few minutes. I'm a good coagulator. It'll stop on it's own. Do you have any tissues? A clean cloth?"

"I don't know." I look in the back. Nothing. Open the glove box. Find a paper towel. "Will this do? Not very sanitary. But it's unused."

She grabs it from me. Folds it up. Presses it over the gauze. I have the feeling she's done this before.

I want to ask her why. Why she would do something so stupid. But she doesn't need my judgment right now. So I ask, "What do you want me to do?"

She hands me the plastic box. "There's some tape in there. Tear off a couple of pieces. Long enough to hold this in place."

I do what she asks. "Want me to—"

"I'll do it." She takes the tape. Sticks it over the gauze and paper towel. Presses against the dressing with one hand. Goes through her backpack with the other. Pulls out a shirt. The one she wore yesterday. "Help me pull my shirt off."

"Um, sure." I tug at it. Try to avert my eyes.

"I could use your help with the other shirt."

I help her get the shirt on over her head. It's hard not to

ogle at her body. But the blood. Her scars. They keep my mind from going where it shouldn't.

She leans back into the passenger seat. Closes her eyes. Keeps her hand under her shirt. "Let's go."

"Are you sure?"

"I said I'm okay. It was just a mistake. No big deal."

"No big deal? Really?" I start the engine.

"Leave me alone." Her voice wavers.

I look over my shoulder and pull into traffic. "Sorry. I have no idea what you're going through."

At least she's stopped acting so nervous. She sits quietly with her eyes closed.

"Does it calm you down?" I ask. "Is that it?"

"Partly," she says softly.

The city skyline comes into view. "You need to tell me where to go."

She sits up straighter and looks around. "A little farther."

Ten minutes later we're off the highway.

I glance at Brooke. She's not holding her stomach anymore. "Did it stop bleeding?"

"Yeah."

She directs me to a neighborhood with big trees. Big houses. They're old but well kept. Neatly mown lawns. Trimmed bushes.

"There." She points to a house on the left.

I turn around and park in front. The house is two stories. Beige and green with broad steps leading up to a wide porch. I don't know much about houses, but the word *stately* comes to mind.

"I'll wait here," I say. "Until you know she's home."

"You can come in."

"I should probably get going. I've got Jethro and everything." My dog's on his feet, wagging his tail. Itching to get out. He could use some water and real dog food. "Is there a park nearby? A grocery store?"

Brooke opens her door. "There's a park up the next street. East a few blocks."

"Brooke?" We both look over. A woman's trotting down the brick walkway toward the pickup. She looks about my grandma's age, only thinner. Taller. Stately, like her house.

"Gram," Brooke murmurs. They meet on the sidewalk. Fall into each other's arms. Hug. Cry.

I grip Jethro's collar so he doesn't jump out the open door.

The hugging and crying goes on for a while. Then the woman holds Brooke by her shoulders. Looks into her eyes. "I'm so glad you're all right." She tucks a strand of blue hair behind Brooke's ear. That's when she notices me. "Who's your friend?"

Brooke looks over. All her sharp edges are gone. As if she finally feels safe. "That's Logan."

"Logan," the woman says. "Would you like to come in?"

Not really. But I don't want to be rude. "Sure." I reach over and close the passenger door. "I'll just be a minute," I tell Jethro. He yelps. I feel bad for him.

I reach the sidewalk. The woman sticks out her thin hand. "I'm Claudia."

We shake. "Nice to meet you."

She wraps her arm around Brooke's shoulder. "Come in. I want to hear all about your adventure." They walk toward the house.

I hear a noise in the pickup. Jethro paws at the window. "I really should take care of my dog first."

"You can bring the dog inside," Claudia says.

"He's not a house dog," I say.

"Well, the yard is fenced. Use the side gate. There's a bucket back there if he needs water. We'll see you in a few minutes."

I watch them as they disappear through the front door, still holding on to each other. Brooke's grandmother seems nice enough. But something tells me I should have kept driving.

Chapter 12

I have a hard time keeping hold of Jethro while I attach his leash. He jumps out of the pickup and runs to the closest tree. Pees forever. Trots from tree to tree. Up and down the street. So many plants, shrubs, and grass. Not a tumbleweed in sight. Must smell really strange. It's strange to me, and I'm not sniffing.

We get back to the house. I open the side gate. It's a tall wooden thing, painted the same colors as the house. I walk Jethro into the backyard. Make sure there's nothing he can destroy. No way for him to get out. I find the faucet and fill a metal bucket with water.

I look around some while he's drinking. It's like a park back here. Perfectly mown lawn. Lots of flowers in the ground and in pots. Upholstered patio furniture. Hot tub. Huge stainless steel grill. A deluxe wooden play set with swings and a slide. I'm guessing that was for Brooke.

"Be good," I tell Jethro. "Stay off the furniture. And

stay out of the plants." I take off his leash. He runs around sniffing, tail wagging. Good thing he already peed.

I hear a tapping sound. Claudia stands at a glass door, waving for me to come in.

I do.

There's a small glass-top table in the center of the room. Potted flowers are scattered around. Orchids, I think. The table is set with fragile-looking cups and saucers. Pastries of some kind on a fancy plate. Brooke's not here.

"Brooke is taking a shower," Claudia says. "She wanted to change out of her dirty clothes. Would you like a cup of tea?"

"Tea?"

"I'd offer you something stronger. But I don't think you're twenty-one yet. How old are you?"

"Eighteen. Water is fine."

"Water. Certainly. I'll be right back. Help yourself to a scone. They're fresh." She leaves through an arched doorway.

By *scone,* I guess she means the pastries. I take one. It crumbles as I bite into it. I try to catch the crumbs with my hand.

She returns with a pitcher of water. "Please, Logan, have a seat." She hands me a small plate from a side table.

"Thanks," I mumble as I sit. Set the pastry on the plate.

Claudia sits across from me. She glances outside. "My, your dog is energetic."

I follow her gaze out the door. Jethro's rubbing his nose

along the lawn. Then he rolls onto his back. Kicks his legs in the air. Starts over again. "Sorry." I move to get up. "He's not used to grass. I'll put him back in the pickup."

"No, no," she says. "It's just a lawn. No harm done."

I don't quite believe her. But I settle back onto my chair.

"So tell me what happened," she says. "Where did you meet my granddaughter?"

I wish Brooke were here. I don't know how much she wants me to share.

"Don't worry," Claudia says. "I know she's a handful. You found her hitchhiking?"

"Sort of. She came into my store. The place my grand-parents own. I work there. It's in Arizona."

"Arizona. I see. And did she shoplift?"

Um. Wow. I don't know what to say. I take a long drink of water. My mouth puckers at the taste of lemon.

"Never mind," she says. "Why did you decide to give her a ride? Oklahoma City is a long way from Arizona."

"I guess I felt sorry for her. Didn't want anything bad to happen."

"That was very gallant of you. And you drove straight here?"

I pause. "No." I decide to leave it at that. Not mention the motel. I don't think she trusts me, no matter what the truth is.

She sips her tea. Narrows her eyes. It suddenly hits

me how much trouble I'm in. If that's where Brooke and
this woman want to take it. I'm eighteen. Still don't know
Brooke's age. But she's young enough. Statutory rape. It
would be her word against mine. "I should get going." I
push away from the table. "It's a long drive. Would you tell
Brooke goodbye for me?"

"He didn't touch me, Gram." I twist around. Brooke's
standing behind my chair. Damp hair. Clean white shorts.
Pink shirt.

"I didn't say he did." Claudia's eyes soften. She beams
at her granddaughter. "You look one hundred percent better.
I think Logan should have dinner with us and stay over-
night. Don't you?"

"If he wants to," Brooke says.

"I really shouldn't," I say.

"Of course you should," says Claudia. "A meal and
good night's sleep is the least I can do. You helped my
granddaughter. Maybe saved her from a terrible fate. And
this way you can start fresh in the morning."

I think about it. If I stay the night, I can drive straight
through tomorrow. Won't have to waste money on a motel
room. "Well, okay. That's really nice of you." Then I
remember Jethro. "Can you tell me where there's a grocery
store? I need to buy food for my dog."

"Does he like roast beef?" Claudia asks.

"He likes all meat."

"There are leftovers in the refrigerator. I'll have Missy cook him some hash."

"That's okay. You don't have to—"

"Nonsense." Claudia stands. "I'll tell Missy. And let her know about dinner. And then, Brooke, I'm calling your mother to let her know you arrived safely. Do you want to speak with her?"

Brooke shakes her head quickly. "Tell her not to come for me. I don't want to see her for a while."

Claudia seems to consider this. "All right." She leaves.

Brooke sits at the table and devours a scone. "I was starving. Missy makes the best pastries."

"Is she a maid?"

"The cook. Betta is the housekeeper." She looks out at the backyard, crumbs on her lips. "You didn't expect all this, did you?"

I shrug. "I wasn't expecting anything."

"Right." She drops three sugar cubes into her cup. Pours tea from a flowered pot. "A girl with a rich grandmother, shoplifting and hitchhiking."

"Okay, maybe it is a little weird. But just because she has money doesn't mean you do."

"Actually, my parents are loaded. My dad's a surgeon. Mom has a huge trust fund from my grandfather. We live in La Jolla. My bedroom has a view of the ocean."

I stare at her. "I'd like you to pay me back for the bus ticket."

"I can't. I'm broke." She laughs. "You should see your face right now. You're totally confused."

She's right. I am.

Chapter 13

Claudia returns before I can find out more about Brooke's money situation. "Why don't you come with me, Logan? I'll show you to your room. I'm sure you'd like to rest and freshen up."

She leads me to the second floor, to the end of a long hallway. The room is huge. Sunny. Frilly curtains. Striped wallpaper. "The bathroom is through there." She points to a door adjoining the room. Huh. My own private bathroom. "Do you have clean clothes?" she asks.

"No. I left in kind of a hurry."

"You and my granddaughter both." She sighs. "Not really thinking, were you? Leave your clothes outside the door. I'll have Betta clean them for you."

"There's no need."

"Dinner is at seven." She steps away. Turns back. "What did Brooke tell you about her history? You were together for many hours."

I shrug. "Not much." I'm sure as heck not bringing up the cutting. "I don't think she likes talking about herself."

Claudia nods. Closes the door behind her.

I sit on the bed, relieved to finally be alone. I flop onto my back. But the bed is too comfortable. I'll sleep if I don't keep moving.

I take off my clothes. Pile my pants, shirt, and socks neatly outside the door. Hold on to my underwear, embarrassed. But I can't stand the thought of wearing them again. So I add them to the pile.

The shower is white tile. Clean. Shiny. The water from the ceiling showerhead falls like rain. I stay in there a long time.

The towel is the size of a beach towel. Thick. Soft. I want to marry it. I return to the bedroom, still drying off. Someone's laid a terry cloth bathrobe across the bed. I open the door a crack. My clothes are gone.

Guess there's nothing I can do until they return. So I lie naked on that big cushy bed. Go instantly to sleep.

◌

I wake up to someone knocking. "Who is it?"

No answer.

I throw on the robe. Open the door. My clothes are neatly folded in a wicker basket. I carry them inside. Put them on, still warm from the dryer.

I look at the clock next to the bed. Six thirty. I get my phone. Not much charge left, but should be enough for a call.

"Hello?" Dad answers.

"Hi, Dad."

"Logan!" His voice cracks. "Where are you?"

"I'm on a road trip. Grandpa told you, right?"

"No! No one told me anything!"

"I told him," I hear Grandpa say in the background.

"You did?" Dad says away from the phone.

"Dad?" I say. "How are you?"

"I'm okay. But Jethro's gone."

"He's with me."

"He is?" Dad says. "Why didn't you tell me?"

"I told him," Grandpa says.

"Dad," I say. "I'm driving home tomorrow. But it will take about twelve hours. So I'll be late. Tell Grandpa."

"Okay. I will."

"No, tell him right now."

I hear muffled voices. Then the line goes dead. I look at my phone. Still some charge. Dad must have hung up. I rub my face with my hand. I never should have done this. He's totally freaked out that I'm gone.

There's a soft knock. Brooke opens the door. She's wearing a dress. She looks older. Younger. I can't tell. Definitely softer. Prettier. I think about saying so. Decide against it. Don't want to give her the wrong idea. Like I'm interested.

"It's almost time for dinner," she says. "Gram hates when people are late."

"I'm ready."

We walk down the hallway together.

"Who were you talking to?" she asks.

"My dad."

"Is he hard of hearing?"

"No. Sorry. Sometimes I feel like I have to shout to get through to him." I glance at her. "How are you?"

She shrugs.

"Glad to see your grandmother?"

"Yeah. Mostly." She looks around the house. "I always liked it here. Mom's flying out tomorrow."

"I thought you didn't want her to."

"I don't. But she doesn't care what I want. She told Gram she's taking me on a vacation to the Bahamas. To get my mind off *things*."

"The Bahamas? That sounds cool."

She rolls her eyes. "Awesome."

We arrive in the dining room. The table is set with a tablecloth. Really nice dishes. I'm afraid to touch anything. Claudia's not here.

"Do I have time to check on Jethro?" I ask.

"A couple of minutes."

I go to the backyard. Brooke goes with me. The dish that must have held his hash is empty. He's stretched out on a chaise lounge. Raises his head when he sees me. Beats his tail slowly.

"Hey! Get down!" I scold him.

He obeys. Slowly.

"I told you to stay off the furniture."

He wanders over to Brooke. She pets him.

"Disloyal mutt."

"Come on," Brooke says. "We'd better go in."

ଔ

Dinner is … interesting. I guess it's chicken. But it's stuffed with something. Buried in a thick sauce. Barely cooked vegetables. Scalloped potatoes. Those I recognize. Grandma makes them all the time. Though not with cheese that tastes like this. It's good. Just different.

Brooke and Claudia do most of the talking. About old times. Things they did together. Places they went. Old friends of Brooke's. But I can tell there's a lot they're not saying. About Brooke running away. About her mom coming. About what happens next. Maybe the light talk is because of me. Or maybe it's a dinner rule—*nothing unpleasant shall be discussed at the table.*

They must run out of safe topics because Claudia shifts her gaze to me. "So, Logan. Did you just graduate from high school?"

My mouth is full and I nod.

"And you're off to college in the fall?"

I swallow. "I'm going to keep working at the store."

"Oh, really? It's a lucrative business, then?"

Lucrative. I think that means it makes money. "Well, it supports all of us."

She asks me about *all of us*. I describe my family.

"So you'll be inheriting the store from your grandparents?"

"I've never really thought about it. But, yeah. I guess."

"An interest in business would seem a prerequisite. Whether you pursue an education or learn on the job. Are you at least drawn to business management?"

I push scalloped potatoes with my fork. I don't know what to tell her. I work. I take care of my dad. I've never looked more than a few weeks into my future. "I haven't really thought about that either."

"You must have *some* interests."

"He likes taking care of people," Brooke says.

"You could be a physician," Claudia says. "Psychologist. Teacher. Preacher." She sniffs. "Seems you have some exploring to do."

She makes it sound so easy. Like I have a choice.

Chapter 14

I set my fork down. "There's nothing wrong with work."

"Of course not." Claudia pours herself another glass of wine. "The world needs laborers." She does that sniffing thing again. I get it. I'm low. Meaningless. Not worth her time. "Save room for dessert," she says. "Missy made blueberry cheesecake."

"Yum," Brooke says.

"Sorry, but I have to pass." I wad up my cloth napkin. Set it next to my plate. "I'm really tired. And I have to leave first thing."

"Are you sure?" Claudia asks.

"Yeah. Thanks for dinner. I may not see you in the morning. So thanks for letting me stay the night." I glance at Brooke. "I hope everything works out."

She gives me a look I can't read. Maybe I could have yesterday. But I'm not sure who she is now. She seems like a different person here.

Claudia rises from the table with me. "Just a moment, Logan." She steps to a side table. Picks up an envelope. "Thank you again for taking care of my granddaughter." She hands it to me.

"What's this?"

"For gas."

"That's not necessary."

She pushes it at me. "I hope you sleep well."

I sigh. Take the envelope. "Thanks." I look one last time at Brooke. I won't be seeing her again. "Bye."

She stares at her dinner plate.

I head upstairs to the guest room. Close the door. Throw the envelope on the bed. Turn on the TV. They must have satellite. I flip through a zillion channels.

I mindlessly watch a movie. Think about Brooke. Wonder what I was expecting from her. She's never expressed any gratitude. Any hint that what I did mattered. And I thought that would change tonight? I'm an idiot.

I turn off the TV. Notice the envelope. Figure I should transfer the cash to my wallet. I open it. Inside are eight one-hundred-dollar bills.

Eight hundred dollars.

What the heck?

This is too much. Way too much. My first thought is to give it back. But I know Claudia will insist that I keep it. Why is she doing this? Is she paying me for my labor? For driving Brooke? If that's the case, she doesn't get it. She doesn't understand people doing something just because it's the right thing to do. I feel sorry for her. At least now I know where Brooke gets that attitude.

I shove two bills in my back pocket—for the gas and last night's motel room. I leave the rest in the envelope and set it on the dresser. Then I climb into bed.

ভ

I'm in the back seat of the old SUV, watching the passing countryside. It's early spring. Late-winter rains have turned the hillsides green and gold with poppies. Mom's driving. She and Dad are arguing. Dad's face is red. Mean. So is Mom's. Whatever he's yelling at her about, she's not backing down.

Why can't they look outside? See how beautiful it is. How perfect. Why are they always mad at each other? I clamp my hands over my ears. "Shut up!"

Mom looks at me in the rearview mirror.

"Shut up!" I yell again. "Shut up! Shut up! Shut up!"

The SUV swerves. Mom screams.

ভ

I sit up, panting. It takes me a second to remember where I am.

I step into the bathroom. Drink a glass of water. Try to make my heart stop racing. I get back into bed. I'm too hot and throw the covers off. Press my palms against my eyes. Try to push the images out of my head. But that never works. The nightmare plays over and over.

I hear a click. Then a floorboard squeak. The room is dark, and I can't see far. "Who's there?"

"It's me." Brooke's voice.

"Is something wrong?" I'm only in my underwear. Quickly pull up the blanket.

"I want to say goodbye." She crawls into bed with me.

"Whoa!" I jump out the other side. Back away. "What are you doing?"

She laughs. "You're such a coward. You'll never lose your virginity this way."

"I thought you just wanted to say goodbye."

"And this is how I'm saying it."

Oh God. All the reasons I'd been telling myself to leave her alone are gone. I can't remember a single one.

She pats the bed. "Come here."

I slowly return. Sit with my back to her. Grip the edge of the mattress. Can't shake the vague sense that this isn't right. But why isn't it right? What harm will it do? She says she's not a virgin. This is her idea, not mine. Seth would tell me I'm a dumb ass to pass this up.

I lie down, facing her. My eyes find hers in the darkness. She's holding the blanket under her chin. I stroke the back of her hand with my finger. "How old are you? Really?"

"Does it matter?"

"It does to me."

She sighs. "Fourteen."

I go to pull my hand away. She grabs it. Holds on. Laces her fingers through mine. "I like you, Logan. No one has ever treated me as nice as you do."

"You hardly know me."

"You hardly know *me.*"

"Exactly. Which is why—"

She leans in. Kisses me. I let her. Damn it. Her skin is as smooth as I imagined. Her lips soft. Gentle. I pull her against me. Kiss her harder. She's like a bird in my arms. A tiny, fragile bird.

All the reasons for leaving her alone suddenly rush through my mind. She's just a kid. We don't have protection. And she is fragile. That cutting. The way she acts. I don't think she's emotionally stable. I gently push her away. "You need to leave." I hear the heaviness in my voice.

"Why?"

"You just do."

"God, you really are a Boy Scout." She jumps out of bed.

"Brooke, wait."

"What now?" She sounds angry.

"I respect you. That's why we can't do this. I'm not rejecting you."

"Oh yeah? It doesn't feel that way." She leaves.

"Brooke." I get out of bed to follow her. But I reach the door and stop. I can't explain myself any more than I already have. She'll just have to get over this.

Chapter 15

It's four thirty when I wake up. Still dark. I get dressed. Tiptoe downstairs. Don't want to wake up Brooke or her grandmother. Make things any more awkward.

I'm hungry. Think about stopping in the kitchen. There's got to be a box of cereal somewhere. But McDonald's is good. I need to get out of here.

Jethro's standing at the glass door. He's wagging his tail. I go outside. "Hey, doggie," I whisper as I click on his leash. "Let's go."

I lead him through the side gate. He leaps into the pickup. Heads directly to the jump seat. I pat the passenger seat. "You're with me today. No company." He happily moves up front. Sits with his back straight, looking out the window.

I stare at the house a second. Wonder which room Brooke sleeps in. Wonder if I did the right thing last night. If I'd had unprotected sex with a fourteen-year-old girl, I think I'd be feeling pretty crappy right now. And I don't feel crappy, I feel fine. So, yeah, I did the right thing. I'm sure Brooke has figured that out by now too.

"My time will come," I say to Jethro wistfully. "Let's go home."

He whacks his tail against the seat.

I drive out of Oklahoma City. Relieved to see it grow smaller in the rearview mirror. Stop at a McDonald's drive-through. Buy a large coffee. Three Egg McMuffins. Give one to Jethro. I'm just pulling out of the driveway when my phone rings. I pull over. Quickly answer it before it dies. "Hello?"

"Logan?" I think it's Brooke. But she sounds strange. Breathy. Like she's barely awake. "I did something stupid. I need you. Logan ...?"

The line goes dead. I look at the screen. No charge left. "Crap."

What was that all about? What stupid thing did she do? My mind flashes to her razor blade. Did she cut herself? What if the cut was too deep? By accident, or .... Would she do that on purpose? Because of last night? A wave of guilt slams me.

I need to warn someone. Claudia. But my phone's dead. I don't know Claudia's phone number anyway. Or even her last name. I pound the steering wheel. "Crap!"

I head back to the highway. Drive east. My stomach knots, threatening to send my breakfast back up. I agonize the whole time I'm speeding. What am I doing? This is not my problem. She has family to take care of her.

But what if they don't know? What if it's my fault?

I pull onto her grandmother's street. An ambulance is parked in front of the house. Cop cars with their lights flashing. My heart pounds. I automatically roll the window down a crack for Jethro. "Stay here." He whines as I close the door.

I run to the house. The front door hangs wide open. I step inside.

Loud voices upstairs. A cop downstairs. "Who are you?" he asks.

"I'm a friend of Brooke's. Is she okay?"

"What's your name?" He gets out a pad and pencil.

"Logan Monroe."

"How do you know her?"

"Why are you questioning me? What's going on?"

There's a commotion on the stairs. We both look up.

Emergency techs carry a stretcher. My breath catches when it comes closer and I see Brooke's face. Her pale skin. Closed eyes.

"Is she okay?" I ask as they lower the wheels.

They roll her toward the waiting ambulance without answering.

"You!" Claudia stands at the top of the stairs glaring at me. Blotches of red stain her bathrobe. Her cheeks are flushed. She's down the stairs in a second. In my face. "What did you do to my granddaughter?"

"Nothing." I step back.

"You must have. She cut herself. Almost bled to death. Would have if I hadn't heard her talking to you on the phone."

I can't tell her Brooke wanted to have sex with me last night. That I told her no. She'll never believe me. "I was thirty minutes out of Oklahoma City. Brooke called. She sounded strange. I didn't have your number. So I drove back to warn you something might be wrong."

Claudia presses her hand to her forehead. The redness drains from her face. I think she believes me.

"How bad is it?" I ask.

"They're not sure yet." She staggers into the living room. Sags onto the arm of a chair.

"Ma'am?" the cop asks. "Anything else I can do?" He looks at me.

She shakes her head. "Thank you, Officer."

He asks for my phone number before he leaves.

Claudia gets to her feet. "I need to call Brooke's mother. Change my clothes. Go to the hospital." She's talking to the air, not to me.

"Did you know she cuts herself?" I ask. Brooke may

hate me for this. But someone needs to know. She needs help. "Not just today," I add. "All the time, I think."

Claudia lowers her eyes. "I thought she'd stopped. Like I thought she'd stopped shoplifting. That's what she and her mother told me. I should have known they weren't telling the truth. They never do."

She gazes out the still-opened front door. "As soon as she's out of the hospital, I'll get her into another treatment program. Near me, this time. So I can keep an eye on her. Her mother …" Her voice trails off. She squares her shoulders. "They don't have a good relationship. That's probably what upset Brooke. She just wanted time away from her. But my daughter wouldn't listen."

"Which hospital are they taking her to?" I ask. "I'd like to visit."

She shakes her head. "Absolutely not. This is a family matter."

I open my mouth to argue.

She holds up her hand. "Enough." She walks to the door. Stands there, waiting for me to leave. "I paid you a nice sum. Be happy with that."

I gape at her. "I don't understand."

She stands there.

I walk out. Stop on the porch. "Can you at least tell her hello for me? That I got her message?"

She closes the door.

It doesn't matter. I've got Brooke's number on my phone. I'll call her when it's charged.

I get in the pickup. Lean my head back and take a deep breath. Jethro gives me a worried look. I pat his head. "It's okay. At least I think it is."

Chapter 16

I drive through Oklahoma. Then Texas. I'm in a daze, worrying about Brooke. The highway is a blur. Four hours go by. I see a billboard.

T-REX!
FOSSILS, GEMSTONES, AUTHENTIC INDIAN JEWELRY!
GAS, WATER, AIR!
FRESH CINNAMON ROLLS!
20 MILES, EXIT 382

There's another sign two miles later. Another two miles after that. I don't need gas, but I do need to pee. And the ads remind me of home.

The last T-Rex billboard comes up. *Exit Now!*

I pull off the highway.

It's a small place. Six pumps. Someone's built a life-size T-Rex next to the store. Must be made of concrete. The

pea-green paint is chipping. Lots of graffiti. *Tom + Emily.*
Kurt Cobain 4VR.

The poor dinosaur looks more sad than scary.

The station sits among pine trees. A few houses nearby.
Post office. Except for the scenery, it's not all that different
from Ferris.

I go inside. Use the restroom. The store's arranged a
little different from ours, but not much. Women's and kids'
clothes near the restrooms. So women can browse while
they're waiting in line to pee. Souvenirs on the way from the
restroom to the counter. Their thing here is rocks and fossils.
Big boxes of colored stones. Geodes. Petrified wood.

I head to the cooler. Grab a water for Jethro and one for
me. A bag of chips. A chicken and cheese sandwich. I'll
split it with Jethro. And a cinnamon bun. Probably made
this morning, so not all that fresh at three in the afternoon.
But it looks good enough.

Out of habit, I glance up at a fisheye mirror. A guy
is standing behind the counter. Looking back at me and
frowning. That's because I'm a red flag. I might be using
the mirror to shoplift. Keep track of employees.

I set my stuff on the counter. "Hey," I say.

"Hey." He's older than me. Maybe mid to late twenties.
Still frowning.

"This your store?" I ask.

He eyes me. "No." He starts ringing up my order.

"I work at a place down in Arizona, on I-10. Kind of like this one."

"Uh-huh." He bags my stuff.

"How long you been working here?"

"Ten years," he says. He takes my money. Gives me change. "One of the only jobs in town. I've got a kid and wife to take care of."

"Yeah, I get it." I take the bag. "Thanks."

"Sure."

An older man steps behind the counter. Says to the guy, "Men's room needs toilet paper. Then Sue can use your help in the back."

The guy leaves. Does what he's told.

I return to the pickup and walk Jethro. Pour him a cup of water. Feed him half the sandwich. Think about the guy in the store. How he already has crow's feet. Frown lines. Stooped shoulders. A beer gut.

I get back on the highway. Think again about the guy in the store. Then about Brooke for the hundredth time. Wonder if she's okay. And I think about Dad. Hope I get home before he goes to bed.

My chest feels heavy for some reason. Tight. I turn the radio up loud. It doesn't help. The heaviness doesn't go away.

The last two hours are the worst. My butt hurts, and I keep fidgeting. My eyes are sore. Jethro knows when we're getting closer. He sits up. Pays attention. Gets to his feet when I pull into the driveway. Whines. Wags his tail. I let him out. Open the gate. Barney barks next door. Jethro barks back.

Bark.

BARK!

Bark.

BARK!

I fill his water dish from the hose. Open the back door. Pour him a bowl of kibble. Step inside. "Dad?"

The TV's on, but he's not on the couch. I check the clock. It's after nine. Almost his bedtime.

"Dad?" I check the bedroom. Bathroom. He's nowhere. I start to panic. Did he go outside? Trip over something? I run out the front door. Hope I don't find him on the ground, injured. Unable to get up. He's not in the front yard or the back.

I go next door and knock. Grandma greets me with, "Logan! That was a short vacation."

"Have you seen Dad?"

"Is that my boy?" Dad calls from the living room.

I take a relieved breath. Step inside. He and Grandpa are sitting together on the couch watching TV. I hear gunfire. Must be a cop show. "Hi, Dad. Hi, Grandpa." I take a good look at Dad. He seems okay. Relaxed.

"You missed dinner," Grandma says. "But there's leftovers. I can heat something up for you."

"That's okay, I'm not hungry. It's after nine. I should probably get Dad home."

"Have a seat, Logan," Grandpa says. "We're in the middle of a program."

"I don't know. Dad?"

"Sit down," he says. "I want to finish this."

Grandma comes back with bowls of ice cream. The sugar will keep Dad awake. Might affect his mood. But he digs into it like a little kid, so I don't say anything.

It's late when I finally get him home. He brushes his teeth. Changes into his pj's. I turn out his light. "Goodnight, Dad."

"G'night."

I go to my room. Plug in my phone. Lie on my bed. My very own bed. It feels like more than two nights since I last slept here. It feels like a lifetime.

Chapter 17

I take my charged phone with me to the store. All morning I wonder if Brooke is still in the hospital. Or if she's at her grandmother's house. Or if her mom's got her on a plane to the Bahamas already. Or maybe she's at a treatment program. I wonder if she even has her phone with her.

It's a busy morning. The store is packed the second I start my shift. Dad's at the registers with me. He seems okay today. Better than usual, in fact. I should feel good about that. But it makes me wonder. Am I not taking care of him as good as my grandparents? Am I doing something wrong?

I finally take a break at eleven. I walk down near Geronimo's last stand. It's just a small cave with a rope across the opening. A plaque describing Geronimo's life. How he hid from Mexican and American soldiers and then attacked them. Inside the cave are pottery shards. Bows and arrows. A fire pit. A mannequin dressed as an Apache. None of it's real. People steal stuff all the time. We just replace it.

There's a bench near the trail. I sit and get out my phone. Brooke's the last person who called. I press her number. The phone rings. Rings a few times more. Maybe she doesn't have it. Maybe it's not charged.

Then someone answers with, "Hello. Who is this?" It's not Brooke's voice. Doesn't sound like Claudia either.

"I'm Logan. Is Brooke there?"

"Logan. This is Brooke's mother. How do you know my daughter?" She stops talking. I hear voices in the background. Can't make out words.

"Logan? This is Claudia."

"Hi. I'd like to speak to Brooke."

Silence. Then, "She's gone."

Gone. As in dead? My heart freezes. "What?"

"Actually, I was about to call you. She ran away from the hospital early this morning. Is she with you?"

It takes me a second to wrap my head around this news. "No. I drove to Arizona alone. That's where I am now."

She's quiet. Probably wondering how she can check out my story. "Do you have any idea where she may have gone?"

Yeah, I do. To New Orleans, to find Anthrax and join the Bashing Pancakes. I should tell her that, but I don't know for sure. Brooke could be anywhere.

"Well?" Claudia asks.

"I don't know where she is."

"If you hear from her, will you please call me? Use this phone number. Now I must go. I have other people on her phone to contact."

"Sure."

"Logan," she says. "You left six hundred dollars in the envelope I gave you. Why?"

"Um … you wouldn't understand." I end the call.

I sit on the bench. Imagine Brooke on the highway, thumbing for a ride. I fear for her. Getting to know her didn't change that. She's still a kid. Still vulnerable. But she has a mind of her own. And there's nothing I can do for her right now.

The heaviness comes back. The tightness in my chest. I don't know what it is. I feel like I can't take a deep-enough breath.

A family hikes down the trail. A dad and mom. Three kids. They stand in front of the cave. The dad reads the plaque aloud. They're quiet for a second. Then one of the kids says, "This is really lame."

"Yeah," the dad says. "Pretty much."

They march back up the trail.

It *is* lame. I almost feel like I should apologize. But for what? This roadside attraction wasn't my idea. I just work here. I get to my feet and slowly follow them.

ଔ

"Logan?" Grandma asks. "Your customer asked you a question."

I focus on the guy on the other side of the counter. "Sorry. What?"

"Can you give me fives and ones?" he asks.

"Sure." I give him his change. He leaves. Finally, there's no one in line.

"You feeling all right?" Grandma asks. "Seems like you're not all here."

"I'm okay." I'm just thinking nonstop about Brooke. About why it feels like something inside me isn't working right.

Melody walks into the store. She's wearing shorts. A tank top. Hannah's not with her. "Hi, Logan."

"Hey." Seeing her lifts my mood.

She heads to the cooler. Comes back with a Dr. Pepper. Snickers bar. Sets them on the counter in front of me. "Please don't say anything."

"About what?" I ask.

"About me going off my diet. I'm sick of boring food."

"Why would I say something? You're perfect." I can't believe I just said that. Grandma snorts next to me.

Melody smiles. "Well, thank you, Logan. That's sweet of you to say."

My cheeks heat up. "So, um, where's Hannah today?"

"With Mom. I needed a break." She gets a panicked look on her face. "Don't get me wrong. She's a good baby. I love her to death. I just—"

"I get it. No need to explain." I finish ringing her order. "Three twenty-four."

She hands me a five-dollar bill. "Seth called last night."

"Yeah, he texted me about an hour ago. Seems like he's having a good time."

"I hope not too good." She winks.

My heart flips. I hand her the bag.

"Well, see you later," she says.

"Yeah. See ya." I stare at her as she leaves. Get a blast of courage. Know I'd better act on it before I change my mind. "Grandma, do you mind—"

"Go ahead," she says with a smile.

I run after Melody. Catch up to her on the other side of the pumps.

"Hey, Melody?"

She stops walking. "Shoot, did I forget something? I'm always leaving things behind."

"No. I just wanted to … I wanted to ask if you want to hang out sometime."

"Hang out?" She narrows her eyes.

"Maybe go for drive. Dinner. Something."

"You mean like a date?"

I'm too embarrassed to answer.

"You're only eighteen."

"So?"

"And you're Seth's best friend. You've been hanging

around the house since you were five. You're like my brother. My kid brother."

I feel like she just slugged me and patted my head at the same time. Even so, I don't want to give up. "I'd look after you. You and Hannah. I wouldn't leave you. I'm not like Josh Becker."

She reaches out and touches my arm. Her eyes are full of pity. "That's sweet of you, Logan. Really. But I'm okay. I don't need looking after." She glances toward the road. "I'd better go."

I watch her for a moment. Then head back to the store.

Chapter 18

The last hour of my shift drags. I find myself glancing up at the mirror a lot. Looking for shoplifters, I guess. Every time I look, I catch sight of myself. I'm always frowning. Like that guy at the T-Rex station. I wonder if I'm growing frown lines already.

Bev and Alex finally replace us.

I drive Dad home. Pull into the driveway.

"It's Friday," he says. "Are you going out?"

I look at him, surprised he remembers what day it is. "No."

"When I was your age, I was out every Friday and Saturday. Your mom liked to dance. I was always driving us up to Tucson. El Paso. Las Cruces."

"Really?" I had no idea. He never talks about his past with Mom.

He opens his door. "Great times."

Maybe his meds are kicking in.

I watch him. Make sure he gets into the house okay.

Then I grab the mail from the box. Give Jethro water and food. Go in through the back door. Dad's at the kitchen table reading the newspaper.

"What do you want for dinner?" I ask.

"Aren't we going next door?"

"I don't know. Are we?"

"They invited us. Dad's trying out his new grill."

"Are you sure? You know how he is. It takes him forever to get the coals started. We won't be eating until midnight."

"It's a gas grill. I want to go."

"Well … okay. Want a snack?"

"Not now. I'll get something if I need it."

I go to my bedroom. Sit on the edge of my bed. Get out my phone. There's no one to call. I don't want to text Seth again. He's got better things to do. I think about Melody. I was such an idiot, imagining she'd ever be interested in me. I hope she doesn't tell Seth. I'm ashamed enough as it is.

I look through the mail. Bills. Ads. Nothing from Mom.

Something Brooke said pops into my head. She'd asked if I'd ever gotten Mom's side of the story. Did I know for a fact she didn't care.

Of course she didn't care. A caring mom would never leave us. I've never doubted that. Not for a second. That's why I haven't opened her letters. Because no matter what she's written in them. No matter what excuses she's given. I won't believe her. And I'll never forgive her.

It's also a fact I've never thrown a single one of her letters away. Why? That makes no sense. It's stupid.

I open the drawer. Grab the envelopes. There must be thirty cards and letters. I carry them outside. Take the lid off the trashcan. Dump them inside. Slam the lid back on.

ଓଃ

I'm quiet at Grandma and Grandpa's that night. They ask for details about my "vacation." I tell them a partial truth. That I drove to Oklahoma City.

"Oklahoma City?" Grandpa says. "Why on earth did you go there?"

I shrug. "Never been there before. Wanted to see it."

He shakes his head.

We finish eating. "Logan," he says. "Will you come help me clean up?"

I follow him to his new grill. He starts scraping off burger gunk. "Isn't she a beauty?" he says.

"It's nice."

"I've been wanting to talk to you, ever since graduation. It's about the store. We want you to be a part owner."

"Really?"

He nods. "Then when we die you'll own it outright. Not that we plan on doing that anytime soon."

I hate thinking about anything happening to them. "What about Dad?" I ask.

"We've set up a trust fund for him." He glances at me.

"This is only if you're interested. Running that place is a lot of work. A big responsibility. You're tied to it day and night. Every day of the year."

"I know."

"No, you don't." He sighs. "You have options, Logan. Don't agree to this because you think you have to. You know I keep bugging you about seeing your mom."

I roll my eyes.

"There are colleges in Tucson. Opportunities. People your own age. Ferris has never been a big place. But when I was young, it at least had a little more to offer."

I shake my head.

"Just think about it." He points at some dishes. "Take those dirty things into the kitchen, will you?"

ෆ

I sleep like crap that night. Watch Dad closely Saturday morning at breakfast. He still seems pretty good. "Did you take your meds?" I ask.

"Yeah, I took them."

I tap my spoon against the edge of my cereal bowl.

"Something on your mind?" he asks.

"I was thinking about going for a drive today."

"You just got back from a drive."

"I know. I'll be here tonight before bedtime. I promise."

I call Grandma and Grandpa. Tell them the same thing.

"Where you going?" Grandpa asks.

"Out."

He hesitates. "Okay. Have fun."

I don't plan on it.

Jethro whines at me through the fence.

"Not this time, doggie. Sorry."

I get on I-10. Head west.

Chapter 19

I memorized Mom's address a long time ago. It's on all of those envelopes I just threw out. I know exactly where she lives too. I found her house the first time I drove to Tucson by myself. Now, every time I'm here I drive by her place.

The small yard is full of cactus. Even a twenty-foot saguaro. I've wondered if that's why she chose this place. She remembered taking me to that park. How much I loved the cactus people.

Sometimes I just drive by. Other times I park across the street. I don't stay long. Don't want to see her or her to see me. I'm not sure why I come. Maybe I want to imagine what her life is like. Grandpa says she hasn't remarried. She works at an elementary school.

Right now there's a car in the driveway. A small white one. A ding in the back fender. I'm guessing it's hers.

I sit in the pickup. And sit. Ten minutes. Fifteen. It's so hot. I've got the air on. I need to make a decision soon. I think about what I might say to her. The hundreds of questions I need to ask. No, just one question.

Why?

I shake my head. No. No way. I can't do this. I reach for the ignition.

A movement catches my eye. Someone's walking out of the house. She stands on the porch. Hands at her sides. Staring back at me.

It's her. It's her. She looks the same. Exactly the same.

My eyes fill with tears. Damn it. Where did they come from? I quickly wipe them away. She looks. Waits. Waits for me to make a decision.

Oh God.

I open the door. Get out and cross the street.

ଔ

I start at the community college in two weeks. I'm nervous about it. Brooke crossed my mind when I had to declare a major on the enrollment form. She'd said I like to take care of people. I guess I do. So I chose psychology. We'll see. Maybe I'll change to business. Take Grandpa up on his offer. Run the store some day. If nothing else, the college is swarming with people my age. Including girls. Lots of girls. It gives me hope I'll find someone.

It was a rough couple of days with Mom. Me shouting. Both of us crying. Even if I don't agree with what she did, I think I at least understand. She and Dad hadn't been getting along. She wanted to move out of Ferris. Get a good job. Get me in a better school. They fought about it all the time.

Then the accident happened. She felt guilty. Thought it was her fault. Said she felt like she was about to explode. Thought I'd be better off with my grandparents instead of her.

"I was a mess," she said. "Not fit to be your mom or your dad's caretaker. It took me a couple of years to straighten myself out. By then you were too angry to let me back into your life." She took a deep breath. "I never stopped loving you, Logan. And I never meant for you to take care of your dad. I thought your grandparents would do that."

I had to admit, that's what Grandma and Grandpa had expected too. I just stepped up. Took it all on myself. Thought that was my job. Or maybe I was just angry with Mom and that was my stubborn way of showing it.

Once I got the anger out of my system, Mom asked if I wanted to stay for a while. See if we could get to know each other again. I agreed and worked it out with Dad and my grandparents.

Now I split my time between Tucson and Ferris—three days with Mom, four with Dad, working at the store. When school starts, I'll work and stay with Dad on the weekends. He's doing pretty good. Getting used to the change in routine. I think he's better off without me hovering so much.

Has to do more on his own, including feeding Jethro. I've had to learn to let go of my old routine too.

It's early morning. I'm in the pickup driving east on I-10, heading for Ferris. The *Geronimo's Last Stand* billboards start showing up. Yeah, they're lame, but they make me smile.

I pull off at the exit for the store and park in the back. My phone dings. It's a text. And a photo.

The photo is of Brooke, a smirking smile on her face. She's wearing a blue cap. The one I gave her from the store with Geronimo on the front. The text reads, "Greetings from treatment in Oklahoma City. It sucks but I'm ok. One of these days I'll thank you for real."

I laugh. Text back, "Glad you're ok. You're welcome."

Want to Keep Reading?

Turn the page for a sneak peek at another book from the Gravel Road Rural series: M.G. Higgins's *Finding Apeman*.

ISBN: 978-1-68021-062-0

CHAPTER 1

Convoy's house reeks. I could get high just standing in his living room. I look around while he's filling my order. Hundreds of plants on makeshift sawhorse tables. Grow lights. Fans. Classic hard rock thumping in the background.

I've been here a few times. It's still impressive. He's got an outside grow too, hidden under the redwood trees. Or so he tells me. The location is secret. He doesn't want people ripping him off.

"Here you go." Convoy emerges from a bedroom. He hands me a paper sack. With his long beard, fat belly, and overalls, he looks like Santa Claus. Or maybe Santa Claus's grungy brother.

"Thanks." I take it from him.

"Almost trimming season," he says. "Want a job?"

"Maybe." My friend Eric told me trimming pays good, but it's tedious. And I'm always worried about getting busted. There's a California medical certificate tacked to Convoy's living room wall. This is clearly more than what's legal. I'm nervous. "So, see ya," I say. Then I head to the door.

"Hey, Diego," he says. "Got a minute?"

"Not really."

"Come on. I want to show you something. You'll appreciate this."

I take a breath. I want to leave. But I'm curious enough to say, "Okay. A minute."

I follow Convoy's wide butt down a long hallway. Turn to the right. He stops in a small room pasted on the back of the house. That's typical for the old houses around here. Lots of add-ons. What's not so typical is what's in the room. Beakers. Bunsen burners. Scales. Chemicals. I glue myself in the doorway. Don't want to get any closer.

"What is it?" I ask, although I have a good idea.

"Meth." Convoy grins. "I'm branching out."

"Is it safe?" The lab looks sloppy to me. Like it could blow up any second.

He shrugs. "It's safe if you know what you're doing."

"Don't you make enough money with weed?"

"There's never enough, son. I'm supporting an ex-wife and four kids. Anyway, how much more trouble can I get into?"

He has a point. But now I'm even more nervous. "I have to go."

"I've got some ready," he says. "Nice quality." He pulls

two tiny bags from his pocket. White powder sparkles inside. "Try it. Give one away. Let me know what you think about it."

"No thanks."

"Are you sure? It will sell itself."

"Yeah, I know. I'm just ... I'm not into it," I say.

He shrugs. "Suit yourself."

I'm out of there. Convoy's pit bull and Rottweiler follow me down the front steps. I forget their names. I'd pet them, but I haven't figure out if they're friendly or just pretending. I shove the bag of weed into my backpack. Ride my bike down Convoy's gravel driveway to the dirt road.

It rained this morning. The road is muddy and slick. Redwood trees tower over me, filtering out the sunlight. It takes all of my focus not to slide and take a header.

A mile later I reach the paved highway. The emerald forest turns into pastures. I ride past dairy farms. Sheep farms. Goat farms. The cheese factory where my aunt works. Into the town of Seton, where cows, sheep, and goats way outnumber people.

I park my bike next to our duplex. Lock it to the gas meter. I want to keep the bike in my room, but my aunt births a cow (heh) when I get mud in the house.

I head straight to my room. Rummage in the corner of my closet. Toss shoes and my soccer ball off the old wooden toy box. Slide it across the floor. Pull the sandwich bags and scale out from under a stuffed tiger and an old Xbox. Convoy bought the scale for me. After I explained my aunt and dad would not understand why a seventeen-year-old needed a scale.

I set a clean sheet of drawing paper on the floor. Carefully measure out several one-ounce bags. I like this part. It's like a meditation. Weigh weed. Seal weed in sandwich bags. Layer bags in toy box. It gives me time to think. Not always a good thing. But I do it anyway.

I think about Convoy and his new meth lab. Seems like a risk, but what do I know? He's right. He's already in major trouble if he gets busted. He's also right about meth selling itself. Lots of kids at school use it. Adults too. People who buy my weed often ask if I can get meth for them.

But no. No way. I'm afraid I'd like it. Get hooked. Anyway, I don't need a lot of money. Just enough to support my weed habit. Buy a few art supplies. Save for tuition to art school.

My phone dings. It's a text from Tanya. "U home? I'm alone XOXO <3"

I text back, "Cool. See u in a few"

My task done, I set aside two bags. One for me, one for Tanya. I put the remaining weed and scale in the bottom of the toy box. Put the toys back inside. And return the box to the closet. Layer the shoes and ball on top. Close the door.

Shake the scraps of weed from the drawing paper onto joint paper. Add more from my baggie. Roll it. Stick it in my pocket.

I walk down the block to Tanya's apartment. Give her a freebie bag. Sit on her bed. Smoke the joint. Get blissfully high. Listen to a new song she downloaded. Talk about stuff. Laugh. Eat pork rinds, the only snack food in her family's kitchen.

I sketch Tanya's portrait on the inside cover of her notebook. I love how her dark brown hair curves in this perfect arc around her cheek and under her chin. And she gets this pouty look that's sexy and evil and innocent, all at the same time. I hold the drawing up for her when I'm finished. "What do you think?"

She stares at it. "You made me into a cartoon."

"Well, yeah, what else? But it's a good cartoon, right?"

She takes the notebook from me. Studies it. Slowly smiles. "It's awesome. I look like Cat Woman. Or Batgirl. I'm fierce!"

Fierce. That's it. I lean my head against the wall. Take a deep breath. Life is good.

Then I make the mistake of telling her about Convoy's meth lab. Her eyes grow wide. "He'll start you off for free," she says. "Can you get me some?"

Then we argue. And life isn't so good.

I walk home, my high wearing off.

About the Author

M.G. Higgins writes fiction and nonfiction for children and young adults.

Her novel *Bi-Normal* won the 2013 Independent Publisher (IPPY) silver medal for Young Adult Fiction. Her novel *Falling Out of Place* was a 2013 Next Generation Indie Book Awards finalist and a 2014 Young Adult Library Services Association (YALSA) Quick Pick nominee. Her novel *I'm Just Me* won the 2014 IPPY silver medal for Multicultural Fiction—Juvenile/Young Adult. It was also a YALSA Quick Pick nominee.

Ms. Higgins's nearly thirty nonfiction titles range from science and technology to history and biographies. While her wide range of topics reflects her varied interests, she especially enjoys writing about mental health issues.

Before becoming a full-time writer, she worked as a school counselor and had a private counseling practice.

When she's not writing, Ms. Higgins enjoys hiking and taking photographs in the Arizona desert where she lives with her husband.